EYE OF ATHENA

HOLLY KNIGHTLEY

EYE OF ATHENA

This book is a work of fiction. Any references to historical events, real people, or real places are used fictitiously. Other names, characters, places, and events are products of the author's imagination, and any resemblance to actual events or places or persons, living or dead, is entirely coincidental.

No part of this book may be reproduced, or stored in a retrieval system, or transmitted in any form or by any means, electronic, mechanical, photocopying, recording, or otherwise, without express written permission of the publisher.

ISBN: 978-1-958761-47-2

Edgar Allan Poe works used from the public domain: *Alone, Annabel Lee, Eleonora, Ligeia, Marginalia, Mesmeric Revelation, Premature Burial, The Black Cat, The Cask of Amontillado, The Fall of the House of Usher, The Masque of the Red Death, The Narrative of Arthur Gordon Pym, The Pit and the Pendulum, The Raven, The Spectacles, The System of Doctor Tarr and Professor Fether, The Tell-Tale Heart.* and letter from Edgar Allan Poe to Mrs. Maria Clemm—July 7, 1849 (LTR-323).

Bible: Genesis 2:7-9

Cover design: Marshmallow Designs

For Mr. Edgar A. Poe
with love and admiration

CONTENTS

CHAPTER ONE

The Mirror

1826

Death is not absolute. There is life beyond the black veil if you choose to listen for it—look for it. There are people for whom this veil is thinner than it is for others. And for the chosen few it is lifted. The realm of the living and the realm of the yet to come blur. Reality blurs. The sane mind and all that is madness blurs.

* * *

I ran my hand over the mercury dabbled mirror in the cellar bathroom. The bruises of the looking glass cast their own blemishes over my reflection like lichen banqueting the flesh of a tree. There was something about the quaintness of the space I was drawn to. There was something to be said about the way the black wallpaper, with its tiny daisies, the size of scarabaeus beetles arched over me, culminating in an ebony lacquered ceiling. And there was something about the old mirror that enticed me to come to the cellar, night after night.

Everything here felt more intimate—felt more real. The daisies on the wallpaper smelled more vibrant than the real ones growing outside my family's ancestral home, more special than the collection of rare flowers from all over the world, including: the East Indies, Africa, and England, that Athena kept in the solarium. Their habitat was dark and damp, the gloomiest of all subterranean homes. Only a small crawl space window let natural light filter in, but it was the moonlight these flowers of the night bent toward with a yearning.

We were one of the few families in Richmond, Virginia that could afford such luxuries as an indoor lavatory and having a bathroom in our cellar was the Dahl fortune on parade. More so, that this bathroom had been abandoned. I was the only one who used it now. I was the only one that came down here after the fire of 1821. The fire had ripped through the family vault, laying to ash the remains of my ancestors and killing twenty servants along with my grandmother's twin brother. Others would smell smoke down here in the dank cellar bathroom, boarded up and forgotten about after all that death, but not me—I could only smell the daisies.

This place had become a refuge for me and every night while everyone in the household slept, I'd sneak down to the cellar and gaze at myself in the antique mirror. My grandmother warned me, since I was a very young child, not to touch the mirror or I would go as mad as a hatter and have to be carted off to an insane asylum with all the other bad little children who didn't listen to their grandmothers. Going as mad as a hatter was a fair price to pay to look into it. A real mercury mirror sparkles. It sparkles as if the very stars from the heavens are trapped beneath its glass. The mirror twinkled with life every time I gazed upon myself and touched its winter-like glass with my fingertips.

Oh, how I love that antique mirror with its round top and etched flowers that outshine the daisies on the wall with a luster only cut glass can give. A thin etched line running along the border of the mirror dared me to be as elegant and thin as it was. I knew once I was, I would sparkle like the mirror—be composed of a thousand little stars that would never burn out.

I was on my way. It wouldn't be long now. This mirror would never lie to me. In the moon-kissed bathroom shrouded by dark shadows that tiptoed in from the corners, I looked thinner. The candle burning on the crawl space ledge cast a halo over my darken form. I would've looked angelic if it weren't for my dark hair that ran nearly the length of my protruding spine like a shadowy mane— for there was no such thing as dark-haired angels. Yet, never had I felt closer to God than when I stood in front of the mirror and gazed at my reflection.

The eyes are the gateway to the soul, and it was so easy to peer into mine through my reflection's eyes. Here alone, could I glimpse a truth I could seldom perceive or want to understand. My one eye was as dark as the sea at night and as calm. My one eye was the lightest blue I had ever seen, blurring into the sclera of my eye. Only its small, pit-like pupil commanded attention, a thing it always did. I liked my eyes. Others may have felt maddened when they looked at me, unsure where to focus their attention: on my dark eye, on my pale-blue eye, on my thin lips, on my raven hair.

My eyes were a true reflection of me, more so than the face in the mirror. They exposed my duplicity like two sides of a coin. I was not unlike the Egyptian god Horus—my left eye the morning and my right eye night. But where Horus's eyes gave him power and healing, mine gave me something darker.

My brown eye was large and all-encompassing like the

innocent eyes of a trusting baby fawn. My blue eye, well, my blue eye was the embodiment of all the evil that dwelled in me. It was there, festering behind the skin and bones of my earthly temple—lurking—waiting for its chance to beckon me to my darkest desires. The only inclination of my perverseness could be glimpsed through my pale-blue eye and seldom did anyone look me dead in that eye, including myself.

I positioned my face between the silvery bark flaking from the back of the antique mirror to get a perfect look at myself. I was pleased—very pleased. "You look pretty today," I whispered to my reflection in a voice as frail as my appearance.

I jumped back, banging the back of my knees into the toilet. I was grateful the sound was blunted by the heavy cotton material of my pants. I didn't want anyone to know I was in the bathroom again. I leaned in slowly, my face moving back into place between the mirror's scars. I scraped my fingernail over the mirror where my lips turned up. Feeling silly, I ran my hand over my lips. The mirror was just my reflection after all. I was the real one. It was my face. My lips were the same old, thin lips that looked like a line cutting across my face. They were cold, but they've been cold for a while. It suited them. Lips like mine were never the kind meant for warm embraces. My lips were the kind for listening. Only the tight-lipped made good listeners, and I was always listening.

I gazed at my reflection half in awe and half in frustration. Why did the lips in the mirror turn up like that? Like they knew a secret. I watched them press together as if to speak to me. I leaned my ear toward the mirror. I heard a voice. It was soft and fragile, as if seldom used. I couldn't discern what the voice said, just that it spoke.

I was not surprised tears welled in my eyes. Despite not understanding the voice, it understood me. I was certain of that—

and I was so seldom understood. My nails dug into the blue velvet lining on the back of the mirror as I clutched it with both hands. I had to be gentle now, the bottom edges of the mirror had already cracked and broken off. But I was anxious to make out the words—for us to share something—to share in the secret hidden behind those thin, curved lips. "You can talk to me," I whispered to my reflection in the voice my grandmother used to soothe me when I was a child. "I will listen."

My own voice shrieked in my ears, forcing me to grab my head in pain. "I know what you've done!" The back of my throat stung as sobs fought free. A whirlwind of emotion tore through me. My head felt like it was on fire as I fought to suppress the memory that clawed at the inside of my skull. I had buried it deep inside of me and threw away the key. But, there it came screaming to the surface, the guilt crushing me as if I was trapped under the mirror's glass.

I swooned, leaning on the sink top for support. My dark hair fell over my alabaster skin like strangling vines. The vein in my forehead pulsed with every beat of my heart that sounded in my eardrums like a summons to war. Pressing my lips to the surface of the mirror, a thin sheet of condensation encrusted it, hiding all of my face except my pale-blue eye. I couldn't hide from the eye. Couldn't hide from its cloudy gaze. It was too late. It knew what I'd done. I recalled the sound of blood, how it dripped into the old porcelain sink like a metronome.

CHAPTER TWO

The Beloved Sister

SIX MONTHS EARLIER

My sister finger-combed my long, dark, straight hair. She itched my scalp with just the right amount of pressure before dragging her delicate fingers through each fine strand, taking her time as not to hurt me. Her fingers running down the length of my hair and her body—her beautiful body—so close to mine as she stood behind the chair I sat in, made me feel alive in a way I never thought I'd feel again. It was as if every cell in my body was pulsing, as if together they created this new heart for me that awoke me from a waking death.

Oh, how I missed this little intimacy with my twin more than anything else. As children we would play for hours doing each other's hair and playing dress up. Nothing made me happier than to be locked in our mother's room trying on clothes too big for us. Our tiny faces would poke out from gossamer lace collars and embroidered necklines smeared with rouge and eyeshadow.

Sissy wanted to look like one of the women we'd seen at the playhouse. She'd twirl around in our mother's gowns pretending to be a princess or a faerie. For me, it was much more. When I played dress up, I dressed as my mother. I wanted to understand her. I wanted to know what kind of person she was before she died. Where Sissy painted her face with bold colors and bright red lip balm that made her look more like a carnival clown than a faerie queen, I took my time. I'd methodically paint my eyelids a color I thought would suit a woman with my fair complexion. We were always told how much we looked like our mother, particularly me, and it pleased me to hear it. I'd wondered what the world would say if they could see me with my eyelids painted robin-egg-blue with soft pink cheeks and lips.

I was broken out of my reverie by my sister's gentle voice. It was as soft as the fluttering of a butterfly's wings and just as beautiful. "Your hair's almost as long as mine." Her nail slid down the middle of my scalp in preparation for two braids.

It was true, my hair had grown very long over the four years we were apart. Whereas before, my father would not let my hair grow past my shoulders, Doctor Tarri was more lenient.

When I was admitted to the care of Dr. Tarri, they cut my hair. It was protocol at Westminster Sanitarium for us all to have closely cropped hair, but I didn't care. I acted every bit as crazy as they thought I was. I clawed at them with the nails of a wild animal while my legs kicked at them like a rabid horse. Despite being a small thirteen-year-old, it took four orderlies to restrain me. They sedated me and shaved my hair down to the scalp.

During my first session with Dr. Tarri, he asked me why I resisted my hair being cut. He restated that the sanitarium did that for hygienic reasons and that he had never had a patient put up such a battle.

The answer was simple and after I gave it to him, he made a deal with me: I would not have to get my hair cut as long as I was a model patient and did everything asked of me.

He understood or at least pretended to understand me. A man like that could never really understand someone like me. He thought, after all, that I was there for his help. But I needed no help, I was and am perfectly sane. Still, I let him think he understood the significance I found in my hair.

On the surface it was simple, so maybe he did grasp that. I didn't want my hair cut because my long, inky black hair reminded me of my sister. It was one of the few physical traits we had in common besides us both having one dark-brown eye and one light-blue eye. Keeping it, having it shroud my head like a hood, brought me closer to her as if she was with me through my suffering. And it did. With every inch my hair grew, our bond grew stronger. It was as if she was reaching out to me through the dark tangles, spurring me on to do what I had to do to free myself of the sanitarium.

I knew it before I came to live at the sanitarium, and my time there only confirmed what I felt in my bones, in the very marrow of who I was—no one understood me. Not my father who placed me there, not my grandmother, not my best friend Eddy, not Dr. Tarri, not the orderlies, no one besides Sissy.

I was one of many in a sea of white gowns. If hearing voices was the reason I was sent there, then I would tell them I no longer heard them. But this had to be done gradually, and gradually I did it. I let them think their treatments, and their sessions, and their exercises were working. I had to snake my way through their science and come out on the other side free. I was every bit of that model patient Dr. Tarri wanted me to be and after four long years of playing their game I was released—cured by modern medicine and deemed safe to reenter the world.

I was free to return home to my sister. It was as if I never separated from her, we were continuing where we left off.

"All done," Sissy said, reaching for her small, silver hand-mirror and thinking better of it.

"How do I look?" I asked, inclining my head to her.

"I'll say this, you pull off braids much better than me."

I tugged on the singular braid that fell over her shoulder. It shined at every fold like her hair was made of silk. "I doubt that."

"Well, too bad we can't ask anyone's opinion."

It *was* too bad. But I was sure I made the right decision dismissing my valet. After four years of no privacy, of doctors and orderlies telling me what to do, what to wear, and what to think, I wanted freedom and independence. Sissy agreed, also dismissing her lady's maid. We had each other. We neither needed nor wanted anyone else. Our time together was sacred, not to be shared with those not like us.

Without delay, Sissy took out the ribbon holding my braid in and worked her fingers through my hair shaking the braid loose.

"Thank you, Sissy. This was fun. It's just how it was before I was sent away."

She sighed longingly, moving on to the next braid. "I'm so happy to have you home Ken. I've been so lonely."

CHAPTER THREE

The Flower and the Outsider

I took my old place at the dining room table across from my sister. My father and my grandmother sat at the heads of the table in robust, cranberry tufted armchairs, the kind I imagined the hierarchy in England still used. Actually, the whole assembly reminded me of prerevolution decadence. Sure, this type of seating arrangement would have appeared normal if we weren't sitting at a fourteen-foot-long table meant to hold over twenty people. But it was just the four of us and until tonight, the three of them.

I suppose at one time the table wasn't nonsensical. It was a necessity for the grand revels my grandmother's parents held and she had held, and even my parents had held, that was until my mother died giving birth to my sister and me.

With our birth, all things merry ended at the Dahl House. And now no one came here. The maximum occupancy for the dining hall was met tonight by my arrival home.

While at the sanitarium, I felt like I was there forever, like I was trapped in one endless nightmare. But now that I was home sitting across from Sissy, it seemed like I was never with Dr. Tarri. There was this uncanny falling back into routine that washed over me. But yet, things *had* changed.

The hands of time had touched everything. I couldn't deny my absence. The table had deep cuts in its surface where cutlery had marred it. The varnish peeled up from the table's edges like reptilian skin. It was hard to resist pulling at it, to see what was under it all. The large *Hunt of the Unicorn* tapestry hanging on the wall behind Sissy was sun battered. The rich colors, that had once made the tapestry a statement piece, were washed out. The texture of the fabric was the only thing to note now and even that seemed tattered under a scrupulous eye. My father and grandmother had also faded as if an invisible vampire drained them of their life force. They seemed smaller, older, and their skin possessed the grayish color of a cadaver. But where my father's hair had grayed, my grandmother's hair had remained as dark as night. Sissy and I looked like her, the sole difference being she had two blue eyes that she hid behind thick spectacles.

Time had ravaged everything but my twin sister. She was a flower in bloom at the sweet age of seventeen. When I smiled, she opened up for me as if I were her sun. I thought of the daisies on the black wallpaper in the cellar bathroom and how they reached for light pouring in from the small crawl space window. They craved moonlight, but what they needed was the sun. The idea that I could be that for my sister thrilled me. She had been lonely in my absence and now that I was home, she wasn't. It felt good to be the sun. To be Helios seemed fitting. Both Apollo and he were Greek gods of the sun and of light, that was before Helios embodied the sun. He wore a radiant crown, and I wore a crown of thorns, that would smother all flowers besides my like-minded sister.

I eagerly awaited dinner. Sissy had told me as we tarried before the pocket doors leading into the dining hall, that tonight we were having my favorite.

It had been so long since I had a normal meal, I couldn't recall what my favorite food was or if I even had one. The food served at the sanitarium was always mashed beyond the point of recognition. It was either lumps of green, lumps of white, or brown lumps. Despite the different colored lumps scooped out of a giant white bucket with a stainless-steel scoop, they all tasted the same. I didn't mind, not really. I had no taste for food, only my freedom. I ate just enough so as not to elicit the attention of an orderly.

When I asked Sissy in earnest what my favorite meal was, her answer was less than poignant: "Your favorite is my favorite."

"My favorite is your favorite," I repeated back to her happily. I liked that immensely. I couldn't hide it and I didn't want to. My smile lit up my face with a toothy grin I had retired. It was just another way we were the same.

Shortly thereafter, a yellow-haired servant girl about Sissy's and my age brought our dinners one by one and placed them before us. She was strikingly beautiful with blue eyes, the color of the sky after a rainstorm. Dark lashes hooded her eyes like the clouds you knew came with the rain. I diverted my attention to the dish she served. She removed the silver dome from my plate and waited for my approval.

My favorite was steak with a side of mashed potatoes and a vegetable medley of carrots, peas, and green beans. The steak was rare. Its natural juices flowed out of the hunk of undercooked meat onto my mashed potatoes. I glanced to my sister. She smiled at me, biting into a green bean with a snap.

"Is it to your standards Sir?" the servant girl asked.

"This is not your favorite," a voice whispered to me. "She's not like you."

Momentarily thrown off guard, I answered the voice. "She is." To prove it—to prove Sissy was just like me—I cut a piece of steak and swallowed it, barely chewing the meat before I committed it to my stomach. It had been so long since I had heard a voice, I thought it belonged to another servant or even the girl that awaited my answer as I heard it with such clarity. But no, it was one of the voices from the airspace between the world of the living and the dead that only I could hear. For I knew, *man doth not yield himself to the angels, nor unto death utterly, save only through the weakness of his feeble will.* Spirits of the dead spoke—and spoke often to those who listened.

The servant girl luckily understood my words as 'it is' rather than 'she is' and after watching me take my first bite, left promptly through the pocket door on the opposite side of the room heading back to the kitchen.

Sweat beaded on my brow as I looked down at my oozing steak. I wiped my forehead with the inside of my elbow. I didn't think I could take another bite. When I looked at my steak, really looked at it, I could see the tendons and ligaments that made up the flank of cow sitting on my plate. It was as if being detached from the cow hadn't killed it. It appeared to be wiggling. This persistent undulation only caused more of its juices to flow onto my vegetables. I felt like the piece I had already swallowed squirmed around inside of my stomach.

"You need to cut your hair," my father said.

My head jerked in his direction. I had forgotten he was there. He chewed on a piece of steak as if it was a sole of a shoe. Saliva dripped out of the corner of his mouth like a foaming animal.

Perhaps sensing my blue eye was watching the drool darken the hairs of his mustache, he wiped his mouth with the cloth napkin he had discarded on the side of his plate.

"What?" I asked, my concentration broken by the cessation of his chewing.

"You look like a girl."

These were the first words my father had said to me in four years. I puzzled at them. I had wondered on the carriage ride to my ancestral home if he would be happy to see me. He had only looked at me when I walked up the granite steps to the house where he waited with my grandmother and my sister. It was Sissy who welcomed me home. It was she and she alone who threw her arms around my neck and shed tears of joy. My father remained unmoved through her tears like a gargoyle. I did my best to follow his example. I did not want to give him any reason to send me back to Westminster Sanitarium for Boys. Me, breaking down in tears at my reunion with my beloved sister could be just the thing to send me back from whence I came. Men did not show emotion. Men did not cry. Emotion was one of the five cardinal vowels of insanity. The A E I O U's of insanity as Dr. Tarri used to call it: Anger, Emotion, Illusion, Outburst, and Unbridled Fear.

'E' for emotion. I may not have physically cried when I saw my sweet sister, but on the inside I sobbed. I had gotten very good at hiding; the sanitarium had taught me that.

"I like my hair," I said with no defiance in my tone.

"All the money we spent on that damn nuthouse, you'd think they could give him a decent haircut."

"Not tonight," my grandmother hissed from her position at the head of the table. "It's Kenneth's first night back home. Let's try to get along."

My grandmother was a kind woman. Very kind and

understanding. She had believed me when I told her about the voices. Believed, when I said I heard my mother calling to me from beyond the mirror.

My father went back to eating. Sissy smiled mischievously at me with lips I envied. Where my lips were thin and flat, hers had a natural curve to them that reminded me of the illustrations of angels everyone was so fond of by the German artist Albrecht Dürer.

"All the boys wear their hair long now," Sissy said.

My father leaned back in his chair, squeezing the armrests. His barrel belly was in full view. "Kenneth you are a Dahl, and as a Dahl you have a reputation to uphold."

That statement baffled me more than anything. I would've thought being sent away to an all-boys sanitarium would have shattered our reputation, or, at the very least, mine. Maybe it was covered up, maybe they believed the heir to the Dahl fortune was away at school.

I heard a voice whisper in my ear. It was unmistakably male. It was deep and scratchy. "You're not the first Dahl to enter the sanitarium."

I smiled at my father. He focused back on his meal. He didn't want to look me in the face, more specifically look me in the eyes. I *was* withholding the Dahl reputation after all. I was not the first of my clan made to suffer the confinements of an insane asylum. I *was* a Dahl. And so was Sissy, and so was my grandmother. It was my father who was the outsider. He married into the Dahl family, changing his surname to ours.

What kind of man would do that? For one thing, a man more interested in money than legacy. I wondered what my mother ever saw in him. He was unattractive, so much so, that I couldn't believe it was a different story in his youth. He was cruel and crude—an unsophisticated ruffian.

A ruffian, that sent me away because he thought I was mad. I had been home for less than a day and already the four years of torture at the hands of the doctors at Westminster were for nothing. I had always known the voices were real, that they were not figments of my imagination conjured up by a sick boy, but voices of the unseen guiding me.

CHAPTER FOUR

An Old Friend

I waited by the large window in my room. It spanned the distance between the floor and the ceiling. Little square mullions, painted in a glossy black, divided the glass into panels. I had abandoned my armchair and had been standing there for some time watching the shades of night change as the hour ticked on. Soon everyone in the house would be asleep and I could make my way to the cellar bathroom unbeknownst. I ran my hand up and down the heavy quilted fabric of the drapery; I was anxious. I wanted to be in the bathroom—I wanted to be standing in front of the mirror. From the moment the daisy wallpaper popped into my head at dinner, my desire to go to the cellar had grown exponentially.

In truth, I had wanted to run down to the mirror the first moment I was left to myself, but the servants were watching. They observed me from a distance as if I was some rare, exotic creature too dangerous to approach. I noticed their beady eyes spying on me from the corners of the room and the more daring, glancing at me from the corners of their eyes. Maybe some of the older servants knew I had come from Westminster Sanitarium. I did recognize a few of them—the coachman most notably. He had driven me to the sanitarium and was the one to retrieve me. It was a long ride from Dahl House to Westminster. It was winter then. My head was buried into my chest. I did that not because of the cold but because the coachman continually stopped and got off of his driver's box to check on me. He never said a word. He would just stare at me for a few minutes, making sure to look at me from the side opposite my blue eye, before climbing back to his seat and spurring on the horses. It made me uneasy, this constant need to check on me. What was he checking for? Perhaps he thought I would try to jump from the coach. As silly as it was, perhaps he thought I would hurt him. Whatever the reason for his peculiarity, he didn't let it be known.

The day I left Westminster Sanitarium for Boys he waited by the stagecoach in the same dark wool greatcoat he had dropped me off in, despite the weather not being nearly brisk enough for it. He spoke not one word. He merely opened the door for me and once I was tucked inside the coach's leathery bowels, he closed it. On the ride home he made the same stops, climbing down from the driver's box to look at me. This time, however, I didn't shy away from his glaring stare. Looking away would be an act of guilt, a thing I learned the hard way at the sanitarium. Innocent people do not look away, they have nothing to be ashamed of. This being drilled into my head almost literally, our eyes stayed locked. Shouts from a carriage behind us had broken his concentration, but not mine. The sanitarium had broken my will, but not my mind. My eyes stayed fixed on him, following him until he was out of sight. I was cured. I was innocent. I would not let anyone think elsewise.

I thought it was more than possible this driver may have told the others where I've come from. Maybe he even told them what I'd done to get sent away and now they were all watching with keen eyes to see the lunatic do his worst. Lunacy seemed to be entertainment for the simpleminded and learned man. Visitors to the sanitarium would come and stare at us as if we were an exhibit at a pop-up caravan carnival. The servants of Dahl House must've been very disappointed I did not jump onto the dinner table and throw my food around like a monkey.

The time for waiting was over. I sneaked out of my room, holding the doorknob tightly as I guided it back to its original position without making a sound. I walked in the center of the hall, down the carpet runner that stretched the length of it. The eyes of my ancestors stared down at me from their canvas prisons, where they hung from the picture rail. An Egyptian motif of the ankh, the key to the Nile and the key to life after death, was hand painted above the picture rail in greens and golds.

I smiled back at the portraits of the Dahl dynasty. I was no longer a captive, I was free. I was living a life after a waking death. I wished they could be happy for me. Some of them were. They whispered celebratory cheers as I walked past, others remained silent. I took their silence as an insurgence against my freedom. But they couldn't stop me, no one could. I was already in what my family called the Burnt Wing. It was a wing of Dahl House closed off after the fire of 1821.

The wing was never restored; instead, it was boarded up rather coarsely. A few thin, wooden boards were nailed across the expansive main hall. It was all too easy to duck under them as a child and now I could step over them. The end of the hall was marked by a large stained-glass window that used to serve as the outer wall of a chapel. The chapel, like most of the wing, had succumbed to the fire and had not been rebuilt. The stained-glass window, having a steel casement, survived. However, a crack forked through the Savior, Jesus Christ, in a zig zag wound.

There was just enough light from the moon and stars to backlight the stained-glass. The red jewels that had been placed into the window as blood shone in the dark as if fire burned inside them. Rubies and red gemstones gleamed from Christ's hands, feet, and side. The rubies seemed to flow down his face like dripping blood.

Above Christ's head, constructed of granite, hung the Dahl family crest. Surrounded by Victor's Laurel was the masked knight of the Dahl family. On his shield were three hearts and in the center of the three hearts was a star. I smiled; the brightest star is the sun. What audacious people the Dahls are. We place our family above the Lord and in us burns the sun—the nourisher of life. Yes, I am a Dahl.

Sissy and I were told never to enter the Burnt Wing, but if you tell children never to do something, they're sure to always do it. Right before I was sent away, the Burnt Wing had become one of Sissy's and my favorite places to play hide and seek. It was on such an occasion, I happened upon the cellar bathroom.

The center of the cellar dropped down to what almost looked like a pit, and there it was—a diamond in the rough. The fire had not damaged it. It had passed over and around the bathroom, most likely because the door was shut. Inside, the room was perfectly preserved, including the mercury mirror, the porcelain sink, and daisy wallpaper.

Standing in front of the cellar bathroom door again, after so much time, was surreal. My hands shook. I was not able to keep them steady as I opened the door. I'd anticipated this reunion as much as the one with Sissy. I entered, forgetting how dark it was in there at night. I was in luck nonetheless, moonlight flooded in from the crawl space window washing the room in a reddish fog. The smell of damp and earth rose to my nostrils cleansing my olfactory sense of the smoky odor of the Burnt Wing.

I wasted no time facing the mirror.

I gasped at my appearance. It was the first time I had seen myself in four years. My father and the doctors at Westminster thought the mirrors caused my psychosis. They believed the voices I heard spoke to me through mirrors. That was not true. I told my father the first voice I had heard—I had heard while looking in a mirror. He interpreted my words as he pleased and rid the entire house of every looking glass except the small hand-mirror Sissy kept in her room and the one my father used to shave. None of the staff were permitted to have one. It was the same in the sanitarium. I never had access to a looking glass or anything that could give off a reflection.

No one knew about this mirror. I had kept it a secret—protected it. I gazed in it now bewildered. I had changed so much in such a short amount of time. Surely, four years couldn't work so much change?

The gentle line of my jaw had sharpened to a square. I could make out a few hairs jutting from it. I ran my hand over my chin, there was more than I thought. I pulled them out one at a time, sometimes accidentally pinching my skin. I hated having hair on my face like a baboon.

I trembled; my chest constricted like I was being squeezed in a vice. I was not beautiful like my sister anymore. I had always imagined I looked like her—that my face had the same soft, feminine lines to match my long, dark hair. When I thought of myself, I'd visualized having her face with my lips, which I knew to be a little thinner and less vibrant. But now I could scarcely see her in me.

Time had stolen my softness. I was a man now, and I looked like one. I hung my head. "You're so ugly . . . so so ugly . . ."

I wished I never came to the bathroom. Never saw the truth the mirror had to show me. My eyes lifted to the glass, my breathing labored. *The true genius shudders at incompleteness—imperfection.* I could've smashed it, sending all the little stars trapped inside it flying across the dark room, but I couldn't. Even in the moonlight, I could see the mirror was special and I longed to be admired like it.

"I can make changes," I promised my reflection. "I can make improvements."

CHAPTER FIVE

A Daisy

I was just about to enter my room when a voice stopped me. "Is there anything I can get for you Mr. Dahl?"

I turned on my heels, expecting to see my father in the hall with a servant. Under the illumination of a gas wall sconce, I saw the same servant girl who had brought me my dinner. My father wasn't present. It was only the two of us standing in the long hall amongst the watching faces of my ancestors.

"Is there anything I can get for you Mr. Dahl?" she repeated, expectantly.

"Please," I said, relieved my father didn't catch me wandering the hall and a slew of questions weren't incurred, "call me Kenneth or Ken. Mr. Dahl is my father."

She smiled, her eyes moving to a half-lidded position as if she was about to giggle.

"And uh, no. I . . . uh, I'm fine, thank you." Anticipating being questioned on why I was out of my room if I didn't need anything I said, "I couldn't sleep. So, I decided to take a walk around the house."

"It was too rare, wasn't it?"

"Huh?"

"The steak. It was too rare. You hardly touched your dinner. I told Cook it was too rare, but she insisted she knew best."

I smiled back at her, imitating the one she had just given me. I had learned people like to see themselves in others.

"It appears *you* know best . . . . um, I didn't get your name earlier."

She curtsied as if I was royalty, lifting the two sides of her simple white nightgown and bowing. "It's Athena. Athena Elle Lee."

"Thank you, Athena. Have a pleasant night."

I placed my hand on the doorknob and was about to open it when I decided to steal another look at Athena. She really was a beautiful girl. She reminded me of how I looked before I left for the sanitarium. The curves of her face were soft, her lips thin. Her light eyes shone even in the dim light of the hallway. They were large expressive, blue eyes. Her nose was tiny, the kind you seldom see anywhere else but on a doll. Her long blonde hair was let down for the night and it flowed in ripples that reminded me of the sea.

I inclined my head toward her and nodded before returning to my bedroom.

* * *

The next morning, I woke up to a knock on my door. Before I could get out of bed, Athena slipped in.

"Good morning," she said, whisking a tray over my lap. "You missed breakfast, but I thought since last night's dinner didn't agree with you, you may be hungry."

She removed the domed lid from the tray to reveal a plate of scrambled eggs, diced tomato, fried potatoes, and a slice of toast topped with butter and grape jam. On the side of the plate was a daisy along with a canteen of water and a glass of orange juice.

She placed the tray cover on the small table next to my armchair.

"Thank you." I forked a few pieces of scrambled egg into my mouth. "I didn't realize I missed breakfast."

"You sure did, slept clear through it. Your father has it served at 8am sharp Sir."

"I'm so used to being woken up. I didn't think about setting my own alarm. I suppose it silly of me, but I normally don't sleep so peacefully."

It was true, I'd slept better than I had in the last four years. The general malaise I'd suffered from seemed like the infliction of a nightmare. I felt at home in my boyhood room. Just as I'd felt at home in the dining hall. It was as if I was plucked from Hell and delivered back home.

"It's quite alright. That's why you have me." Athena bobbed in place as if she was floating on water. Her head and body seemed to move out of time. "I'm sure there's a lot of things you're going to have to get used to now that your home from England for good."

So, there it was, everyone believed I was abroad. That was much better than the truth. Lunacy, though entertaining to the masses, holds a stigma that few can look past. I wondered if Athena would've been so candid with me if she knew about Westminster Sanitarium.

"Yes," I said, taking another bite of egg. The little yellow nuggets reminded me of the lumps at the sanitarium, but they tasted better. "There's going to be a lot of little things I'm going to have to adjust to."

I could have eaten the whole plate, but recalling my reflection in the mirror, I put my fork down. I had to pace myself. If I was going to return to a prettier me, I was going to have to make sacrifices.

I sniffed the daisy on my plate, bringing it as close to my nose as possible. The delicate velvet-like petals tickled me. "I love flowers."

Athena smiled at me like she did last night, and I knew not everyone got a flower with their breakfast. Her eyelashes dusted over her cheeks like birds skating over a frozen lake. Athena was stunning in the daylight, more so than by lamplight. The light from my window blanketed her delicate form in a yellow haze. It was as if she, herself, was made of the sun. The light caught pieces of her hair, giving the effect her hair danced in the sunlight.

"I love flowers too. I look after the solarium now. If it pleases you, you should come by. I can show you all of the new flowers."

I smelled the daisy again, wondering if this beautiful creature divined this was my favorite flower. "I think I will."

Her eyes moved to their half-lidded position of last night.

"Will there be anything else Mr. Dahl?"

"Athena," I said, putting emphasis on her name, "I asked you not to call me that."

She flushed; a blotchy red traveled the length of her neck to her cheeks. "Yes, you did, but I can't possibly call you by your first name. If anyone hears, I will lose my station for insubordination."

I reasoned that could very well be true, if my father heard. Dahls had a reputation to withhold after all. "Very well, but when we are alone in my room, please do as I ask."

"Yes of course," she said with such a remorse, I pitied her. I could tell she felt she had let me down, her head drooped on her slouched shoulders like a flower hit by frost. Maybe she wasn't made of the sun. If my words could do that to her, I was *her* sun as I was for Sissy. But I didn't see how that could be, we didn't know each other. Not how Sissy and I knew each other. Not how we understood each other.

I was baffled by Athena's extreme change in disposition. I didn't feel I scolded her. And if our conversation could have been considered a reprimand, it was done politely. After all, she had been very kind to me. I wondered why she would choose to work here if she felt so chastised by my family and me. Clearly a girl of her youth and beauty could find better employment.

I ran my finger down the slope of the silver fork, "Athena, may I ask you a question?"

Her eyes came alive, she was eager to please. "Yes, whatever you like."

"Do you enjoy working here?"

"Oh yes, very much. And if you don't mind me saying so, more so now that your here."

"I don't mind you saying it, but I don't understand why this is. Why would I make working here more enjoyable for you?"

My question caused her blush to continue its journey to the tips of her ears. I wondered if they would be hot to the touch, and desired to run my fingers down her delicate earlobes.

Athena didn't answer me, instead her head drooped again, as if my words were blows, her chin now resting on her chest in an attempt to hide her face.

"Come here," I beckoned with a gesture of my hand. She obeyed, sidling up to the side of my bed. I took her hand, having her take a seat. "Tell me why it is that you like working here more since I arrived."

"I ..."

"Look at me Athena. I'm trying to understand you."

And I was. I had very little experience talking to anyone, especially girls. And everything about Athena puzzled me. Her behavior was so different than Sissy's. It was as if each gesture of her hand, each nod of her head, every flutter of her eyelids had a secret meaning, and I didn't have the key to unlock them. All I had were my questions and they seemed to be getting me nowhere.

"Sir . . . I"

"Ken."

"Ken, I can't," she said, allowing herself to glance at my face before directing her line of vision to my breakfast tray.

"Why is that? Is it because of my eye."

She nodded slightly before burying her chin in her chest again.

"What about my eye stops you from looking at me?"

"I feel like when I look you in that eye, the blue one Sir, my heart whispers my darkest desires to you."

My hand slid up her arm and rested on her bosom above her heart. "Even if I could hear the secret whispers of your heart, I would prefer you to tell me them yourself. I would like to understand you, Athena."

Her head lifted slowly until our eyes met.

"What is the secret desire of your heart?"

In a whisper she told me, "I want you to kiss me."

"Be more specific," I said, also whispering. "Where do you want me to kiss you?"

Her chest heaved under my hand.

"I want you to kiss me everywhere."

I shook my head. "That's too broad. You have to be more specific Athena, if I am to ever understand you. Is it your hand you want me to kiss?"

"Yeesss," she said, her answer trembling like her body.

My fingers slid down her chest, taking up her hand again. I pressed my lips to the top of it. Her hand was so delicate, child-like—it was easily half the size of my own. I liked how it felt in mine. With my lips still pressed to her hand, I looked up at her, my lips breaking their seal on her skin to smile. "Is there anywhere else you want me to kiss?"

Sissy barreled into my bedroom. I released Athena's hand. "There you are Athena." She saw my breakfast and scoffed. "I'd like some breakfast too."

Athena rose abruptly.

Sissy, still in her nightgown, climbed into bed and sat next to me. "I'm eating breakfast with my brother today, bring my tray in here." She plucked a slice of potato off my plate and popped it into her mouth. "Needs salt."

"You better get Sissy her breakfast before she eats all of mine."

Athena stood there for a moment looking at me with her expressive blue eyes. If only I could read them as she thought I could. "Of course," she said, skirting out of the room.

I smiled at Sissy. I wasn't sure, now that I was a grown man, if she would still climb into my bed like she did every morning when we were children.

Athena rushed into my room with a tray for Sissy. She was so quick the tray must have been waiting in the kitchen for her to deliver it. Athena pulled the lid. I noticed no daisy adorned her tray and so did Sissy.

"Where's my flower?"

"Um . . . I . . ."

Sissy waved her hand dismissively. "No matter. Just make sure I have one tomorrow."

Athena and I shared a secret glance. She gazed at me as if I was the one with secrets before slipping out of my room.

CHAPTER SIX

The Barber

I sat in a makeshift barber chair in the servant dining hall. My chair had wooden arms and legs with a fabric seat cushion and backing. This particular chair was chosen because there were three bars in the back that allowed the chair to be reclined by adjusting them. I gathered from Cook's reproachful glances, I was using her favorite chair. If the death stares weren't enough of a tell, the seat cushion was. The cushion was worn in the center thanks to the load of its usual burden and smelled like Cook—a mixture of cooking grease with a twist of lemon.

I found Cook's chair very comfortable and didn't mind the smell, but I did mind being in the servant's dining hall. This was my first time there and would be my last. It had nothing to do with my status.

The servant dining hall was reserved for the working class.

It was the primary point of ingress and egress for servants and where we received visitors who were not affluent. The servant dining hall had received my childhood instructors, and also was where household goods were delivered. As a boy, I'd ventured to the kitchen with Sissy before to sneak a snack, but we never had the need to venture into the dining hall.

I didn't like it there. The room was squat, with a long table that ran down its center, taking up most of the space. There was a hearth to one side and on the other side the labyrinthine system of servant bells that snaked up and through the house. The walls were comprised of the same small, gray-toned stones as the floor. The servant dining hall, as a whole, reminded me of a crypt.

The house *has* a family crypt, we Dahls referred to as The Vault. My mother was the last person to be placed in the family vault before her body was buried on the grounds. I had visited it trying to glimpse a little bit of her. I had left empty handed and vowed never to return to the place. There was something about the air in The Vault that attacked one's spirit. And then there were the voices. They yelled at me—screamed at me to be heard. I couldn't take it.

The little hairs on my arms and the nape of my neck stood on end. I fought the urge to shudder. There was another place that came to mind as I sat in the servant dining hall while the barber applied a thick lather to my face. In Westminster Sanitarium, in the oldest part of the building, there were stone cells used to hold the sanitarium's most uncontrolled psychiatric patients. I had been placed in one of these cells after the boxing match I put on over getting my hair cut. It also reminded me of a tomb; the proportions were just different. It too was made of small stone, the mortar slicked with green algae that extended in tiny, finger-like projections. My hands, if they were not tight across my chest in a straitjacket, would have been able to reach the sides of my prison. In comparison to the servants dining hall, the ceiling at the sanitarium was tall—very tall. I felt like I was trapped in a pit, like I fell down a well. There was a small window high above me that I could never reach.

The light perceived from the small window barely helped to distinguish between night and day, and I gained no advantage of such tells from the iron door to my cell. The air was thick—thicker than the air in my family's subterranean vault. It was sick, like I breathed in my own sour air. I was locked in there for what I believed to be three days, soaked in my own sweat and filth, unable to use my hands and unable to free myself from my restraints to relieve myself. The moisture seeping from the stone was my only source of nourishment. When my spirit was broken, and I was near death, the doctors came for me, and my testing began.

I felt like the walls of the dining hall were closing in on me, the room shrinking with every tick of the second hand of my pocket watch that I now gripped. *There was an iciness, a sinking, a sickening of the heart—an unredeemed dreariness of thought which no goading of the imagination could torture into aught of the sublime.* I was compelled to ask the barber to stop, holding back my desire to throw my hands out like a madman, and asked him with a grace befitting of my family, "pardon me, but the air in here is stifling, may you please prop open the door."

He did as I asked and propped open the exterior door. A faint breeze reached me, and I instantly felt better. I was not buried alive. Life was right outside the stony walls. I felt like the servants were treated worse than the clinically insane, being forced to take their meals here. The idea of Athena, beautiful little Athena, being made to sup here under the oppressive weight of the walls moved me. I was sure if this was to continue, her spirit and frail body would succumb to the weight and inhume her right there in the servants dining hall.

The barber also seemed grateful for the breeze that stirred up the scent of the morning's breakfast. I could smell flour and butter and the aroma of freshly made bread. I could also smell sweat. The barber was sweating profusely and smelled like a rotten onion left out in the sun to further putrefy. I was grateful for the scent of the lather that had a flowery smell, somewhere between rose petals and lavender. I don't know why I'd hesitated to ask him to prop open the door, he'd been stopping every minute or two to wipe his temple with his checkered pocket-handkerchief.

I was unsure why he was perspiring as he did. It wasn't hot in the servant dining hall, but rather the opposite. The dining hall was sunken, a few steps required to enter or leave it. Attributed to being partly underground and being comprised of stone, it was quite cool there, even with the kitchen being just through the pocket doors that were shut for my privacy.

I watched him acutely as his hand, with hairy knuckles that reminded me more of a beast than a man, hovered over the different razors he had spread out on a leather mat.

The razors reminded me of miniature butcher knives with extended handles. They were sturdier than the surgeon's scalpels I'd seen at Westminster. I wanted a set.

The razors, being so close to me, spread out on the table only an arm's length away, tempted me to touch them. Before I could pick a razor up for further examination, the barber pulled them away, almost sending the lot of them to the floor.

"You mustn't touch Mr. Dahl, you could cut yourself."

I sighed, it was a heavy, exaggerated sigh. I hated it when I was called Mr. Dahl. Knowing he, like Athena, would not call me by my first name I said, "Call me Dahl please."

"My apologies Sir," he said, lining the razors up on the leather mat again. "They are very sharp."

"Yes, I see that. I'd like a set of my own."

My request seemed to make the already drenched man perspire all the more. The sweat dripped down his face like a leaky faucet. I had never seen anything like it. Not even on the faces of my fellow patients that had worked themselves into a stupor, had I seen that much sweat.

"Yes, Mr. Dahl, Sir Dahl . . . Dahl. I will see what I can do."

This man appeared to know what I had done to get me sent away to Westminster. It was the only logical explanation for his anxiety. I wondered if he would have come at my request if my father had not summoned him. As my father refused me my own mirror, he had no choice but to call for the town barber. I could not stand the thought of little whiskers on my chin and knew what I had to say to get him to obey: "It maddens me." And just like that the rest of the world stopped what they were doing to accommodate the Dahl family, where we sat high above the town in our glass house.

He feared me; I was sure of that. He shied away from my blue eye as if it was a laser set to destroy him. I regretted this relationship was not going to work out. My father was going to have to hire a private barber to live at Dahl House. I wanted to be shaved twice a day and if the town barber couldn't handle it, we would have to seek other means. I wanted my face to be as smooth as it was in my boyhood.

"I never killed a man," I told the barber as he wiped the remnants of the shaving cream from my face.

He dropped the towelette on the ground. Quickly recovering it, he jammed it in his pocket. "Of course not, Sir."

He didn't believe me. He kept his back turned to me as he packed up the instruments of his craft. I ran my hand over my cheeks and chin. My skin felt soft, softer than I recalled it in my youth.

"You did a very nice job. I'm pleased."

"Thank you, Sir," he said, still not turning around.

Rubbing my chin, enjoying the feel of perfect smoothness, I remarked, "Perhaps being in my presence weighs too heavily on your mental fortitude."

He faced me with his razors in his hands, not armed to use them but more as a sign of his professional merits. His stance recalled me to the tombs of ancient Kings adorned with their likeness, with their scepter in hand crossed over their chest.

I didn't move, but my eyes raked over him, trying to understand his peculiar behavior. He appeared to be an ordinary man, minus his very hairy knuckles. I found that to be his only off-putting variant. His face was closely shaven. A deep groove like a pit sat in the center of his jutting chin. His eyes were round and dark and the hair on his head, though comely, was sparce. His wardrobe was befitting a barber, including a leather apron.

"No Sir, nothing like that. It's just that I've never been called to the house before. It's a huge honor for a man like me."

"Oh," I said, shifting in my seat to cross my legs.

He went on, as if my utterance required him to. "I don't listen to town gossip, that's for women."

I ran my fingers over the varnished arm rest of Cook's chair. "I have no doubt, but I am curious. What is the town gossip regarding my family and myself?"

"Nothing about you Sir, not that I would take stock of a single word of it. It's just the old widows and children whispering. Idle hands spread the Devil's work, that's what my mother always said."

I patiently waited, keeping my eyes on him.

"But uh, back to your question, they say Dahl House is haunted."

I laughed. It was a boom of laughter, springing forth from my stomach. It was the first time I recalled laughing since I was a very young boy. "Haunted, that's exceptionally silly."

The barber seemed in good humor now, spurred on by my laughter. "Yes Sir. They say a little boy used to live here who went mad. They said he heard voices, and those voices told him to do things, bad things."

I stopped laughing.

The barber covered his mouth with his hand, no doubt realizing I was the little boy of the rumors. "Sorry Sir, I didn't . . . I didn't mean to offend you. It's only silly rumors, spread by silly children and lonely crones."

"Well, you've met me, so I ask, what is your impression of me? Do you think I'm mad?"

"Oh no Sir, to the contrary," he said with a sincerity that made me believe him. "I think you are the sanest person in the house. It's not my place to say, so if you would pardon me this rudeness, but you should really have a stern talking to with the cook. She almost took my head off with a ladle when I took the chair you're sitting on out of her office."

I smiled. "Then you wouldn't be opposed to coming here morning and night?"

"If that's your wish Sir, it'd be my honor."

I stood and shook his hand, like I had seen men do since I was a boy. I was not mad. The voices did not tell me what to do. I never hurt anyone, not intentionally. Why were the town folk so cruel? Hadn't I been made to suffer enough over the last four years?

I didn't mean to kill my grandmother's cat. I loved that cat. I cried when I discovered I had smothered Pluto with my caresses.

I didn't mean it. I just wanted him as close to me as possible. His soft, black fur felt so good between my fingertips, his sandpaper tongue tickled me. How I sobbed over his lifeless body. I leaned over him, kissing him on the mouth. "God bless you. Oh, God bless you." For anyone who could love me had to be blessed.

CHAPTER SEVEN

Where the Dead Sleep

It took two tries with two different matchsticks to light the candle I placed in the crawl space window. The air in the basement, being thick and moist, snuffed out the flame before the wick could be lit, but I was persistent. Soon the smell of smoke filled the small cellar bathroom, and a warm glow consumed the dark wallpaper, bringing the daisies on it to life.

The previous night's moonlight had served me well, but with the candle I could see my freshly shaven face in perfect detail. I didn't think I could ever get used to seeing my face again—seeing the slight slope of my nose, the flat lines of my lips, my square chin. I felt like I was looking at a stranger. I had no clue who Kenneth Dahl was. It's a funny thing how everyone sees your face but you. One's own face is hidden to themselves. We are kept in the dark on how we look when we smile, how our lips move over our teeth. We do not get to see the gleam in our own eyes or see how our own eyebrows laugh or frown. So much about a person, their inner workings, the things that make them tick, can be glimpsed by their face. Being withheld from seeing mine for four years stripped away all the things I thought I knew about myself. I was just getting to know me again, more than that—I was getting to see the mask I presented to the world—how people saw me, who people believed me to be. I always knew no one besides Sissy saw the real me, for I wore my face on the inside. If only I could've worn it on the outside, maybe I could have understood everything.

That's what the nocturnal visits to the mirror were about. It was a way for me to understand who I had become—a way for me to come to terms with what had happened to me.

I'd always thought no one besides Sissy and my grandmother's cat Pluto could love me because they didn't understand me. I had a best friend once, I loved him. I thought we understood each other, we had so much in common: the love of Sissy, the love of science, the oppression of a father who didn't love us, but I was wrong. Sharing experiences and interests with a friend does not mean they understand you.

I believe with all of my heart and soul, love comes from understanding. But I wasn't sure I understood myself anymore. I needed to know myself if I was going to survive out of the sanitarium. I understood that with a desperation that kept me in front of the mirror. Now that I was home, I wanted to thrive. I wanted to prove my father and every doctor who ever treated me like I was a danger to others and myself wrong.

When I was satisfied I could recall my face after having my eyelids closed, I was ready to leave. I knew then I had a better grip on who Kenneth Dahl was and was ready for bed. I licked my fingers and put them to the wick. I pulled out my matchbox from my inside waistcoat pocket. Lighting a match, I moved in the direction of my bedroom. I preferred to travel by matchlight, the lit matchstick gave off enough brightness without the conspicuous glare of a candle or lantern. Besides, my eyes always had a sensitivity to lamplight.

I closed the bathroom door, the match flame flickered. I shielded it with my hand. I thought of the barber, who I was very pleased with at the moment. My shave was flawless, the mirror proved that. I recalled what he said about the house being haunted and consequently, the little boy who went mad from hearing voices. I had laughed outright at the idea of Dahl House being haunted, partially from relief that I was not at the center of the town's rumor mill, but I was. I was the little boy of their gossip, but I wasn't mad. I *did* hear voices.

One of the voices, the first one I ever heard, was the voice of my mother. At least I had come to believe it was my mother's voice. And she was indeed dead. By principle, if both points were true: I was sane and I heard the voice of my mother, that *would* make Dahl House haunted. To be haunted or be in a haunted place had such a damaging connotation. The barber, though he said he didn't buy into the town gossip, was evidently afraid to be in the house. All of that sweat couldn't have been the result of gratitude for being asked to the house to shave me. The Dahl's had money and that gave us power, but the man's shirt could have been rung out. Admittedly, he was a little less moist during my shave after dinner, but he still had a nervous energy about him even in the main hall. I'd never thought of my family's ancestral home as haunted, rather I felt I belonged. But there was that one place that unnerved me. The very place that I'd recalled in the servant dining hall with the barber—the family vault—The Vault.

I decided, since I was already in the bowels of the house, I should visit The Vault. I took the servant stairs, as a short cut, shaving off a few minutes. The Vault was directly under the original part of the house. It was beneath the bedrooms and to the right of the servant dining hall.

The family vault had been originally used as a burial chamber; however, in the modern day, it had become a temporary resting place until interment in the family cemetery. After the fire, all of the bones that rested on stone shelves, or in dug out niches were removed from the crypt and buried in Dahl Cemetery.

I made my way down a series of sloping halls passing a few rooms that used to serve as root cellars for the storage of vegetables and grain in the winter. There was even a room used as an icehouse. These had long ago been abandoned with the new additions to the estate. The catacombs were cut off from the house with an iron gate. I found the gate reassuring; it was as if its iron hands held back Death. The gate spanned nearly six feet wide and hit the ceiling. In scrolling letters it read: Dahl. A blacksmith had hammered out large, ornate birds who sat on thorned vines. The vines twisted around the bars of the gate. The steely vines were plentiful with perfectly round iron berries. The craftsmanship was so lifelike it looked like the birds, which I assumed to be crows, could come to life at any moment and gobble down the berries.

A large, iron lock hung from the gate, the key still in it. I remembered this from my boyhood. I'd found this just as puzzling then as I did now. Why was there a lock on the place where the dead sleep?

I twisted the key in the lock and opened the gate, the murder of crows splitting down the middle with a groan. I held my breath at the noise. It sounded loud in the quiet space—too loud. It was true the bedrooms were built above The Vault, but at this subterranean depth I was sure it was impossible for anyone to hear me. There were layers of stone, wood, and plaster. The heavy tapestries and thick curtains provided yet another layer of sound proofing. I exhaled; confident I did not arouse my father to my location.

Before me was a staircase cut from the earth. The crude construction was masked with the same stone pavers that gave the servant dining hall its feudal, claustrophobic quality. I lit a new match, holding it out in front of me. The air was foul, a mixture of mold and smoke pervaded my nostrils. The fire that had claimed the lives of nearly two dozen servants and my grandmother's twin brother had also blazed through the catacombs. The stones were charred with soot, leaving them marred in black.

I descended the stairs carefully. Under the dim light of the match, mineral deposits of nitre gleamed in the darkness taking on the appearance of the red eyes of rats. These beady eyes seemed to follow me, blinking at me with every step like stars in Hell.

The match was hardly up to the task of lighting my way. The flame flickered as a murmur of voices rose. These voices were not the chorus of the unseen rats but something else—something undead. Indistinct as the wind, but ever present, they spoke as if their phantom breath was responsible for the wavering flame.

I struggled to see the next tread in the waning light. A stone under my foot lifted. I wobbled. I threw my hands up and back to try to stop my fall, but it was too late. My foot slid underneath me, and I tumbled down the stairs, the matchbox skidding across the floor as the back of my head struck stone.

* * *

I came to, all was dark. I couldn't lift my arms. They were restrained. I struggled, feeling something weighing me down—straps. It couldn't be.

"It's okay Kenneth," I heard Dr. Tarri say. "This is going to help you. Recall yesterday's lesson—*never to suffer would never to have been blessed.*"

I bit down on the bite block in my mouth unable to speak. Dr. Tarri brushed my hair away from my face with the back of his hand as he always did right before he was about to do something horrible to me.

"Don't cry Ken, remember emotion is one of the five cardinal vowels of insanity. You have to remain in control of your emotions at all times. It's the only way to make the voices go away. You did great yesterday. We're just going to up the amperage one amp. I want you to blink twice when you can no longer hear the voices."

I nodded the best I could, my head was in a vice strapped to a steel table. Metal conductors were secured to my fingers, chest, and temples. I blinked twice. An anticipatory tear of pain ran down my cheek.

A hand brushed back my hair again, however this touch was different. It was soft but cold. So cold. I heard a voice, it was unmistakably female, soft as the touch and as gentle as the breeze on a nice day.

"Kenneth wake up . . . wake up Kenneth . . . you have to wake up now."

My eyes opened. I didn't dare move. I don't think I could have even if I wanted to. My arms, though not restrained, felt just as immobilized. Hovering above me as I lay on my back, was a woman with dark hair. Her black hair and her white gown were explicitly detailed as if I was seeing her under a microscope. Her gown glowed in the dark as if by bioluminescence. The face of the woman, if I can call what I saw a face, was black and shadow-like. It was not viscous or solid but something in between. All of her features appeared to be scraped off as if by fingernails, but there was no blood. Her hands, like her hair and gown, were clearly visible and were small and delicate and as white and distinct as her face was black and distorted.

My heart surged. *The madness of a memory which busies itself among forbidden things,* came rushing to the surface. I had seen this faceless woman before—when I was a little boy. In fact, this had all happened before. I had fallen on the same loose paver and fell down the stairs. I had completely forgotten about it as if it was wiped from my memory. I had fallen, smacking my head against the floor. I recalled the feel of my own blood as it pooled around me—cool and wet. I recalled Sissy screaming from the top of the stairs before running to get help. Sissy was gone but this woman had stayed with me. Unable to move or close my eyes, I stared at her. She spoke my name. It was her voice. The voice that I thought was my mother's. I had heard it long before I heard it through the cellar looking glass and had forgotten.

I wanted to speak—to say something to the woman. But my tongue was thick in my mouth as if I still bit onto Dr. Tarri's bite block. I tried to swallow. "Shh," the woman said, brushing my hair back as she did when I was a boy. A chill ran down the side of my face, down my arm to my chest. It burned. "Welcome home Kenneth, I've missed you."

With great effort, I lifted my hand toward her. Just as my hand was to come into contact with her gown, she disappeared. I was left in complete darkness. The bearing weight absolved, I was free to move. I scrambled for the matchbox, feeling the ground like a blind man. Finding it, I lit a match. I walked it around the room, making sure not to move too quickly for fear of the flame going out. There was no sign of the woman, just the glowing red eyes peering out of the darkness. My free hand went to the back of my head where a sizable lump could be felt, but there was no blood to mark my injury as severe.

I brought the match to the ground, directing the small flame to the foot of the stairs as best I could. A red stain was still visible on the stone floor from my first fall.

I felt dizzy, the tidal wave of déjà vu still washing over me. I couldn't believe I'd forgotten about the faceless woman. I couldn't believe I forgot about being carried out of the catacombs by my father, unable to move or speak. I recalled now with a veracity that consumed me, the countless doctors who came to treat me. I'd been comatose for almost a week, not able to respond to anyone or anything. I was the living dead.

Then one day, unexpectedly as if by a miracle, I awoke as if from a dream. It was as if nothing had happened, I recalled nothing. That day, the day I awoke from my sickness, I heard my first voice.

Completely unaware a week prior I had fallen down the stairs of the family vault, I continued my search for information about my mother beginning with where my mind had last placed me. Unbeknownst to myself and my family, I retraced my every step and ended up at the marble coffin reserved for the newly dead in the center of the catacombs.

As if I was reliving my past, I stood in the center of the catacombs as I had done a little over four years ago. From the centermost point it felt like The Vault's crude walls warped around in a circle, the distinct and individual crypts and niches blurring. There was only one thing in focus. Carved from the whitest marble rested an open coffin on a marble platform. Its brightness, unspoiled by soot.

As a boy, the platform was as tall as I was. Cherubs with blunt wings and chubby faces were painstakingly carved into it. I recalled thinking we would have been the same height if they didn't bend their bodies together like a stream of angels covering the platform. Their hands all pointed up as if they bore the weight of the coffin above.

Standing on my tippy toes, I had run my hand along the casket on top of the platform, trying to get a sense of my mother. I knew she had rested in its marble walls before being put in the ground. I'm not sure what made the thirteen-year-old me think visiting this marble coffin would bring me closer to my mother than visiting her headstone on the grounds, but I did, and I left disappointed, gaining nothing from touching the oblong box or even guessing that I had just been in the family vault and suffered a great fall. I did, however, get the strong impression that this place was not hallowed grounds like the cemetery and that unsettled me. I didn't want to visit The Vault again.

Leaving shortly after, I found myself in the cellar bathroom. I looked into the bathroom looking glass and heard a woman. "Kenneth you're beautiful," the voice had said to me in such a kind way it's hard to describe. But in those few words there was so much meaning, so much emotion and love. I thought it was the voice of my mother. It was everything I had imagined my mother's voice to be. It wasn't long after that I heard the voices stirring from the catacombs calling out to me—beckoning me to come down there and play.

A moment of clarity—a feeling of despair ripped through me, causing me to tremble. The match fell from my hands. I quickly lit another. The voices started after I fell. I did not remember that. Was Dr. Tarri right? Were the voices a direct result of physical trauma? It was my head after all that took the brunt of the fall. He had been right about pain making the voices disappear. After being subjected to pain, day in and day out, the voices were gradually drowned out until I could no longer hear them, not even my mother's voice. I had never imagined myself insane. The idea that Dr. Tarri was right about the voices being a delusion of my sickness, enraged me. The idea that Westminster Sanitarium for Boys was good for me was more than I could tolerate. I needed to prove Dr. Tarri wrong. The voices were real, how I came to hear them was irrelevant.

My heart pounded with rage. "Mother," I said, staring through the match flame as I stood in front of the marble coffin high on its cherub-carved platform. "I need you to answer me. Please, if anyone is here answer me."

Out of the corner of my eye, I saw a dark form move. I spun my match in the direction. The flame burnt down to my finger. "Ouch." I dropped it, wasting no time lighting another.

A cold hand rested on my shoulder as I struggled to light another match. This didn't feel like the soft touch of the faceless woman. It was firm and the cold burnt through me. I turned on my heels, almost slipping on the algae slick floor. I recalled something else. Something significant. My tumble down the stone steps as a boy was not from a loose paver. I recalled a cold grip on my shoulder. I had craned my neck back to tell Sissy to let go but she was at the top of the stairs. Before I could react to that reality, I felt a push.

Getting a match lit, I took the stairs two at a time, my pulse climbing with every passing tread. There was something in the family crypt. Something that couldn't have been my sweet mother. I felt relieved when I got to the gate. With the rapidity of a haunted man, I shut and locked it.

CHAPTER EIGHT

Pallas Athena

I returned to my room to find Athena asleep on my bed. If it weren't for the rising and falling of her chest, I would've thought she had been placed on my bed for final visitation. Her arms were folded over her chest as if she had been lain to rest amongst a sea of my pillows and blankets.

Her white eyelet nightdress just covered her toes. The soles of her feet were exposed. Her feet, like her hands, were small and child-like. Her face was as white as a marble bust and I marveled at its smoothness. She was in distinct contrast to my dark room as the marble coffin had been in the gloom of the catacombs. Her blonde hair flowed over my navy sheets in ripples. The scene drew the parallel of a fallen angel on the Plutonian Shore. It seemed a great injustice that Pluto, the Greek god of the underworld, should have such a beautiful maiden wash up on the shore of the river Styx. If you could even call her a maiden. I questioned her humanity; she seemed more like a goddess. Her own name betrayed her true identity. Could she be the Greek goddess of wisdom and war? Could Pallas Athena be here, on my sheets, on my bed? Her wisdom was visible on Earth through her sleeping body. Her pallid skin and white nightgown were the visible representation of her infinite wisdom. And my room, and me as the sun had long ago set, were the unknown and ignorant in the darkness.

Here in my room, with her eyes closed, she had access to her divinity, and she was seeing me for the first time. I wondered what she saw there—what she saw deep inside of me, in places I was too afraid to look.

There was this uncontrollable shiver that passed through me. The kind you can only get from staying out in the cold for hours on end. My body trembled as it did in the catacombs. Whether it was from the fear that had followed me from the family vault or fear she'd see something in me she didn't like, I knelt on the side of the bed and whispered her name. "Athena."

She stirred. Opening her eyes to see me, she shot up like a firecracker. Afraid I frightened her, I placed my hands on her shoulders. "Be calm Athena, it's only me. It's Kenneth Dahl. You fell asleep in my room."

She looked into my pale-blue eye, getting lost there for a moment. What she saw there, I could only ponder.

"I'm sorry. I came to your room to make sure you didn't need anything before I went to bed. When you weren't here, I decided to wait and accidentally fell asleep. I should have lit a lamp. I'm sorry."

"No need to apologize. It should be me apologizing for startling you . . . I don't want to hurt you." I brushed a loose curl away from her face. That was better. Now I could see her bright eyes, and how they shone. "I'm sorry, Athena."

"It's late, I should go." She broke free of me and moved to the door. Her footfalls were like air, I couldn't distinguish them on the hardwood floor. She turned to me before placing her hand on the doorknob. "That is if you don't want anything?"

I shook my head. And just like that she was gone, slipping through the door like a wraith. She seemed destined to baffle me.

I took a seat in the armchair next to the window, leaning to pull back the purple drapery to get a better look at the moon as I mused over the enigmatic Athena Elle Lee. The moon was crescent-shape and hung oppressively low over the tarn. Its reflection consumed the water's surface painting it in a silvery glow that reminded me of my own reflection in the cellar mirror. I longed to see myself in it again. The mystery of myself, I knew, I could uncover through that most magnificent looking glass. I had just determined to go back to the cellar when I heard a light tapping on my chamber door. It was so faint, I wasn't sure if it was a knock or just the wind. As I was leaving all the same, I got up to check. I opened my bedroom door to see Athena.

"May I come in?"

I nodded more baffled than ever. She really was a puzzle—a beautiful enigma. She entered. I closed the door behind her, returning to my armchair while she tarried by the door.

"What do you want from me, Athena?" I asked, my face covered in shadows, hers illuminated by the silver moon. She looked almost spectral if it weren't for her feet anchoring her to this world.

She pulled on the lace of her collar. "I want to continue our talk from this morning."

"That's the past. If we are ever to understand each other, we have to understand each other in the present."

In a fit of passion, she threw herself at my feet. Rising between my legs like a phantom, she took my hands in hers and gazed into my eyes.

"What do you want from me, Athena?" I asked again, pondering the very answer.

"I want permission to kiss you."

My breathing slowed to shallow breaths. "Explain it to me. I need to know every little thing you're thinking. No matter how small or insignificant you think it is, I need to know it—all of it."

She squeezed my hands trying to comply with my request. "I want to kiss you because no man has ever been so kind to me. No gentleman would ever dare to let the likes of me call them by their first name."

"I need more Athena," I said in a whisper. I tried to be kind to everyone I met. That didn't make everyone want to kiss me.

"Because you were so kind to me, I want to return the favor and kiss your lips."

"My lips . . ." I said in earnest, pulling a hand free and running my fingers over my mouth. "Why my lips? Don't you find them too thin to want to kiss?"

"No," she said, shaking her head almost violently, "I find them perfect. I have never seen such handsome lips. Kenneth Dahl, you look like something out of my dreams."

She confounded me. Her tone was sincere, her body was in supplication at my feet. She meant what she said.

"Do I have permission? May I kiss you?"

"Yes," I said barely audible.

She sat up on her knees pressing her lips to mine. Her lips were soft, like the fleshy inside of a plum. They were different from the firm lips of Dr. Tarri. And then there was so much emotion in her kiss. Tears rolled down her cheeks as if pressing her lips to mine was hurting her. It couldn't possibly be so. My lips couldn't actually hurt her. Why was she crying? With Dr. Tarri things were robotic as if it was another one of his tests. There was never emotion in it.

She pulled herself away from my lips, letting the palms of her hands rest on the tops of my thighs. We were just far enough apart now to gaze into each other's eyes. I liked this. It felt intimate. I liked that she looked me in both my eyes, unscared of what she saw.

"I love you," she said.

My eyebrows arched at the unexpected confession. Dr. Tarri had also claimed to love me, but he didn't. And I knew Athena didn't either. So why did she make such a claim?

"Athena, how can you love me if you don't understand me? If you love someone, you understand them. Like how Sissy and I understand each other."

"I want to understand you," she said, with as much emotion as her kiss. "I want to. Please let me try. I feel like I know you already even if you know nothing about me. Your sister wrote the most splendid stories about her beloved twin brother. I couldn't help but fall in love with you. Don't you see, I loved you before we met. You seemed like a fairy tale prince that I thought could only exist in the stories of little girls. But when you came home, I knew the stories to all be true."

My breathing quickened, my chest rising and falling in quick succession. "I'm not easy to understand. Sissy's the only one who ever has."

"I'll try until I do. I know I can't replace her but let me try."

I smiled, a soft reflection of my hope. "And I will try to understand you too, Athena."

She reached her small face up to mine again; I met her halfway. I had never willingly kissed another living soul. Kisses had been taken from me, my lips becoming rubber under the unwanted tugging and pulling. But my lips had never moved against other lips, never requited the forces applied to them with action or want. With Athena it was different. My lips moved with hers in a dance. It was a perfect waltz.

The dance stopped. Teeth collided with teeth. I was too aggressive. Embarrassed, I backed off. She seemed not to notice or mind and pressed her lips to mine again. I was careful to keep control this time, following her lead and kissing her how she kissed me—slowly, meaningfully—there was no rush, we had all night. This little flower bent toward the moon.

CHAPTER NINE

Heaven in the Tarn

My sister and I enjoyed the morning on a blanket spread out by the side of the tarn. It was a naturally occurring lake spreading out less than half an acre. Its small size mattered not; it took away none of its magnificence. We wouldn't have too many more days like this, autumn was approaching, and would soon turn the leaves gold and red and kiss everything in frost. But for today, it was sunny with only a few puffy clouds in the sky. Every cloud reminded me of the skeletons of dandelion heads. Every passing cloud made me want to make a wish on a blowball, but I didn't believe in such things. I had grown up and believed in next to nothing now, besides my sister. And maybe Athena. Last night in the dark seemed like a dream in the dazzling sunlight. Which life was reality?

I reclined on the blanket, propping myself up on my elbows.

I had been outdoors so few times over the last several years, I could count them on my hand, and I wanted to take everything in. We had the cover of an umbrella, but we didn't need or want it. Sissy had tossed her bonnet aside to bask in the sun's warmth and my hat and I had parted ways while the first ray of sunlight washed over my face.

The sun on my face was euphoric. The warmth on my cheeks, a warmth that felt too good to be good for you, relaxed my body into a state of paralysis. I understood why cats sunbathed as they did, napping all day long. I could've done the same and dozed off if it weren't for the tarn, itself, stimulating my mind.

The water's surface was so still it reflected the blue sky like a mirror. The reflection of the sky seemed infinite, like Heaven was trapped in our lake. My head rested in my palms now, scooting up to the water on my elbows, I stared into it, wondering if I dived in if I would be swimming in water or flying in the sky.

I answered my own question. At the water's edge, the tallest peak of Dahl House loomed over the tarn like turrets of a medieval castle. The house was originally built in the English manor style, a means to a cozy home. Renovation heaped on renovation, extravagance outdoing extravagance, the house became an uneasy spectacle sprawling high into the sky and deep into the earth. It spanned the property taking on the shape of an unlucky horseshoe.

Its reflection was as dark and menacing as it was in reality. The stone bricks were nearly black with age and sin. The windows seemed like the black eyes of a demon watching over us, evaluating our every move. The water that reflected the house was as still as the rest of the lake, but somehow it seemed less at peace against the blue sky. It was a metaphor for my life. I would be drowning in Heaven or falling from its celestial skies. Blue skies like these were not meant for people like me.

I glanced at Sissy. We were so much alike, I hoped we didn't share the same fate. She deserved more than me because she was simply better than me. The best of both of us was in her.

Sissy didn't seem to notice me watching her. "If you're going to continue to scribble in your notebook all day, I suppose I too should keep my hands busy. Perhaps, I should rekindle my childhood fondness for embroidery."

"Idle hands spread the Devil's work," she said.

I took a deep breath. I had heard that . . .

Sissy continued to write in her notebook, not giving another thought to me. It was a small thing, bound in red leather. For as long as I can remember, she carried it with her almost every place she went, always scribbling in it. When it was full, she'd remove the pages and add more. This was no doubt where Athena read Sissy's stories about me.

Sissy had always fancied herself a writer. More to the point, a poet, though she wrote very few things she would ever let me read, and nothing since I've been back. I was a little jealous she had let Athena read her stories, but was grateful she did. Without those stories, Athena may not have fallen in love with me. I had doubted Athena's sincerity when she said it, like any sane man would. We, after all, had just met the night before over raw steak, but she did. She thought I was the boy in those stories—a prince—nay a god of the sun.

My eyes went back to the still water, to the reflection of Dahl House. I wished my thoughts could stay on Athena and the wisdom that came with the light. I should have been able to, it was sunny enough, but my mind went into dark places, back to the catacombs under the house.

"Sissy, do you remember going to The Vault as children?"

Without looking up from her book she muttered, "Yes."

"Do you remember me falling?"

"Uh huh."

I sat up, crossing my legs. "Did you see the woman?"

I got her attention. She closed her notebook, trapping her stub of a pencil in its pages, and looked at me. Her brown eye focused on my face, darting from my lips to my nose and resting on its likeness. Her blue eye seemed to focus on something inside of me.

I attempted to construct what the woman looked like with my hands as I described her. "Her face was dark like it was made of smoke, but yet I could see these scratches."

"You shouldn't have gone down there. Promise me you won't go again."

"But what about the woman?"

She took my hands in hers.

I shook my head. "Oh, that's right, you think like grandmother and father, you think I'm mad."

I had only seen the faceless woman twice and both times after I fell. I could chalk it up to trauma though I felt the uncanny déjà vu moment was more than just coincidence. But then there was that voice. Dr. Tarri hammered it out of my head, blocking it out with so much pain, I no longer heard it, but it was a voice I could never forget. Dr. Tarri may have made the voices go away but that didn't make them any less real to me. I knew what I heard, and I knew I was not insane.

Sissy kissed my knuckles as if to apologize.

I'd give in, I didn't want to go back to the family vault anyway, but all the same, I was going to get something out of her—a little payback for her not believing the voices were real.

"Fine, I won't go back to The Vault, but only if you show me what you've been writing in that book of yours since I've come home."

"Nothing, I can't think of a damn thing."

"Sissy, show me."

She exhaled loudly as she opened her notebook. I grinned at her discomfort, enjoying seeing the blush on her cheeks. She looked radiant in the sunlight with her rosy cheeks and snow-white skin that shined like the lake. She pushed her open notebook over to me. Scribbled across it in frustration as if she was stabbing at the paper, read the words: dam, dam, dam.

I chuckled. "You can't force poetry out that way. Eddy always said it had to flow naturally."

Once upon a time Eddy was my best friend, our best friend really, as I seldom was without Sissy. He was the ward of one of my father's business associates and became a regular visitor. Sissy was impressed with his time spent in England and his mastery of languages, and, in truth, so was I. He was what Sissy called a natural poet. Someone who had it in their soul and in their eyes and everywhere else as far as Sissy was concerned. She had been smitten with him since childhood and strove to emulate him, and I think she was as good, at least as children. Sissy's writing block was far from poetic. I had no word of the outside world in the sanitarium and refused to ask about Eddy Poe, let alone his literary ventures.

I slid my sister's notebook back to her, patting her hand. "I'm sure with that much passion you'll come up with something soon. And damn has a silent 'N' my silly girl."

CHAPTER TEN

The Oval Mirror

I returned from the cellar to find Athena sitting on my bed. I smiled ear to ear. It had been so long since I smiled like that. The sensation felt magical. "I was hoping to find you here. All day I wondered if last night was a dream. It didn't seem possible but here you are, a goddess, sitting on my bed waiting for me."

She rose, taking my hands. Her hair was let down as it was the night before, tumbling in ringlets over her shoulders. Her hair and her face were aglow in the light of the gas lamp. Her eyes were a cloudless blue.

"I have something special for you."

"For me?" I asked, with a palpitating heart. I couldn't recall the last time someone had something nice to give me. Punishments and tests, oh yes, those were given to me with abandon, but something special—no, I couldn't recall.

"I know you're upset your father won't allow you to have your own shaving razors, but I thought you could at least have this."

From a pocket in the front of her night gown, she pulled out a small, wrapped package that fit in the palm of her hand. It was wrapped in brown paper and secured with a bow of twine. I took it from her, the smile on my face glued in place. I unwrapped my gift to find a pin. This pin was very special. A silver braid wrapped around an oval mirror. Great pains had been taken to shine the silver and it shone with a brilliant luster. The pin looked like it originally held a miniature portrait but had been customized for me.

It shook in my palm, catching the light in the room. I could see Athena's eyes in it. Her beautiful blue globes rivaled the heavens with their own twinkling stars. Never before had I seen such lusciously radiant eyes as Athena's that night.

"I know you're not allowed to have a mirror, but I don't see the harm it could do. It's just a little one." She flipped the pin onto its back. "On the inside of the backing my name's engraved. It's perfect, that way if anyone should see you with it, the blame will fall to me, not you."

"I don't know what to say, Athena," I said in awe of my most thoughtful gift.

She smiled a warm smile that illuminated her face like her eyes. "Usually when someone gives you a present, you say thank you."

I folded my hand on top of hers. "Yes, thank you. It *is* perfect."

"Let me see the pin."

I handed it to her. She stood next to me, stretching her hand out so I could see myself in the tiny reflection. "I want you to see what I see when I look at you. You're so hard on yourself, I thought seeing how beautiful you truly are could help. See?"

I took the mirror from her, passing it over my face slowly. Until now, I had only seen Athena's celestial eyes in it. It was strange to me how in the lamp light of the room, in Athena's mirror, I looked differently than I did in the old mercury mirror in the cellar. It was still me in the reflection, but I had changed.

Her lips pressed against the side of my face.

I worried I was being rude, not offering her a glance. With mirrors being forbidden in Dahl House, I was sure she was eager to gaze upon her own beauty. "Do you want to look into it?"

"I don't need to. I can see myself in your eyes."

Yes, that was it—why I looked different. I could see Athena in my eyes. My own deity was there trapped in the windows of my soul. I brought her closer, pressing her to my hot body. Straight away, our lips found each other. She was just as soft as yesterday, and still just as new. She slipped out of her nightgown. Her skin shimmered as if she was made from millions of little stars, like she, herself, was a looking glass. I could see myself with her, in her. I understood why my father forbade mirrors. They were dangerously attractive, springing forth a passion I had never known before.

* * *

"Kenneth, there are three ways to manage mania that have been proven successful: pain, isolation, and logic. You need to understand there may never be a cure for your condition, but we here at Westminster Sanitarium for Boys are dedicated to rehabilitating all of our patients. We provide dynamic, cutting-edge science here that you can't find anywhere else in the world. My personal mission is to help you."

I nodded, looking around the room. This room, more than any other one I had been brought to, unnerved me. It was stark white like most of the rooms but this one was full of blue and white tubing that wrapped around large iron wheels that jutted from the walls. In the center of the room was a metal platform the height of a bed. From each of its four corners stood hollow metal poles. It was one cohesive structure. I wondered if what I was looking at was indeed a metal bed.

Two orderlies, dressed in the same white as the room, walked me toward the metal platform. They pressed my shoulders, forcing me to sit on it, then forced me on to my back. They strapped my arms and legs down. Instinctively, I tugged at my restraints. The leather straps were drawn so tightly, the slightest motion cut into my skin.

Dr. Tarri stood at the head of the platform, looking down at me. I could plainly read his embroidered name on his lab coat and smell his stale breath. His eyes were the cunning black of a demon, growing darker and larger as my fear grew. "Kenneth, pain has been proven to be our most effective agent against mania. Pain helps patients clear their mind. And that is what we will be exploring today. We will be doing an experiment in pain discovery. Our goal is to learn how much pain and what type of pain best silences the voices."

"I don't like pain," I said in a whisper.

"What you don't realize Ken, is that you're already in pain. Your mind is screaming in agony—tortured. Keep in mind we are here to help you."

The orderlies brought over a flat sheet of metal made of the same material as the platform. Through holes located on each corner of the sheet of metal, they slid it over the four posts extending from the platform I was strapped to. They brought the metal sheet down upon my person, forcing me to turn my head to the side. I watched the orderlies bring over a clear tank. They placed it on top of the metal sheet that laid on top of me. They attached tubes to it. The sound of the plastic tubing unraveling agitated my already overstimulated nerves. Dr. Tarri turned a small, blue-painted wheel on the far wall and the tank began to fill with water.

I could hear the rushing water as it compounded its weight on me. I struggled to free myself, but already the weight of the metal sheet above me and my restraints proved too much.

"It's okay Ken," Dr. Tarri said, running his hand over my freshly cut hair. "This is for your own good. I will be able to tell when you no longer hear the voices, and when we hit that precipice, the water gets drained. I want to build our relationship on trust, so please, don't insult my intelligence and say you don't hear them. I can tell you do. You have all these little tells that a trained psychiatrist can pick up."

I stopped squirming, the pressure of the water was oppressive. My head and chest ached. "I can't breathe," I whispered to him. "Please . . . I can't breathe."

Dr. Tarri knelt by the side of the metal platform, his hot breath blanketing my face. "*Words have no power to impress the mind without the exquisite horror of their reality.*"

* * *

"Ken, wake up, you're having a nightmare."

Athena continued to shake me until my eyes flashed open. I rolled onto my back, my skin hot with sweat. I focused on my breathing, each breath I took, becoming easier. I had a bad habit of sleeping on my side and would sometimes end up rolling onto my stomach. Every time I did that, the pressure of my own body on my chest brought me back to that moment.

Athena put her head on my shoulder. "What did you dream of?"

I ran my hand down her arm, reassured I was back home in my own room with the goddess of wisdom and war. She would protect me. "A test . . . when I was away, I had to take many hard tests."

"Did you pass?"

"No," I said breathlessly, "but I think that was the point."

She craned her swan-like neck, pressing her lips to mine. "I will never test you, Ken."

CHAPTER ELEVEN

The Prodigal Poet

Four months later

Sissy and I made our way to her favorite spot. Having lunch in the center of the hedge maze had become a tradition since my arrival back home. At the center of the maze sat a stone table with hibiscus leaves and little cherub heads carved into it. A canopy of wisteria, bare from winter's bite, hung over us.

It was much different from my favorite place. There, light filtered into the cellar bathroom in a narrow beam focusing on my mirror; here, everything was sun doused. The strangling vine couldn't shut out the sun though it tried, its twisted tendrils clung to every inch of the arbor it could latch onto.

It suited her—the sunlight—the open space. I again felt that we were different, and it worried me. I wanted us to remain as much alike as possible. I never wanted her to outgrow me and leave. I feared above all things, she would move on and leave me behind.

But I took solace in the cold. It suited her and it suited me. Her complexion looked more stunning with rosy cheeks. Being kissed by the cold made her look more alive.

It may have been her who looked livelier in the cold, but I was the one who felt it. I preferred the pain of the cold, the way it made my joints ache verses my usual numbness of body. It made me feel alive in ways other pain had sucked the life from me. There was something pure about the cold. Maybe because it came from Mother Earth, maybe it was the fresh smell in the air that seemed to cleanse you from the inside out, or maybe it was because the cold, unlike other pain, would eventually kill you peacefully.

But not all cold is good. Not all cold comes from Mother Earth. Science can be cold too, and it could kill you just as peacefully. I distinctly recalled the day I was escorted into the laboratory, a room covered floor to ceiling in white-square tiles. This was where the patients of Westminster were hosed off after tests, if need be, and where we were corralled for monthly baths. Being brought to this room was troublesome. My day had just started, no tests had been administered, and I was relatively clean. I was ushered past the bathing station to a door I had never noticed. It was camouflaged into the wall, also plastered in white tile. The door opened into a small room. This room was an extension of its larger counterpart and was also clad in the same tile, but in its center was a large soaking tub filled with water. I held back a smile. We had soakers like this at the house and I longed to have a bath, to sit in hot water and relax. I was finally getting rewarded. I knew I had done well with my test yesterday, but this was unexpected.

Dr. Tarri came through a door on the opposite side of the room. My invisible smile disappeared.

"Good morning, Ken. Hope you slept well."

"Good morning, Dr. Tarri."

"Well," he said, gesturing to the tub, "today we're moving away from pain as a treatment for mania and moving into isolation. Being submerged in the cold water will help you clear your mind. The water will mute your senses. You will not be able to see, your hearing will be muffled, and your body will be weightless."

An orderly untied the back of my gown. It fell to the floor. I did my best to cover up as I approached the edge of the tub. I dipped my hand into the water. "It's cold."

"Yes, I believe I said cold water."

"I'll catch a cold and die."

"No Ken, that's an old wives' tale. There's no science to that. Now, get in."

I nibbled on my bottom lip.

"We can do this the easy way Kenneth, or the hard way."

"The easy way," I said, stepping over the threshold of the tub. I stood knee-deep in water, my kneecaps clapping together. I wrapped my arms around my torso forgetting about modesty. "It's freezing, Dr. Tarri."

"It's ice water Ken, it's supposed to be freezing."

He motioned to the orderlies. From opposite sides of the tub, they gripped my shoulders.

"Sit down, Ken," he said in an unremarkable tone. He didn't put emphasis on his words. He didn't have to. He knew I, like all the patients at Westminster, would do what he said.

I sat; my teeth chattered. Before I could protest, I was dunked under the water. My arms and legs flailed. I was pulled up, gasping for air. My heart beat in my ears as if it was ready to explode.

"Kenneth, you have to remain calm for this to work. Let go. Let the cold in."

At his command, the orderlies pushed me under the water again, and again I came up gasping.

Dr. Tarri gently moved my damp hair from my face. "Ken, this will all be over the moment you relax, do you understand?"

I was pushed back under. I tried not to move my limbs—tried not to resist the hands that held me down. The cold water was penetrating. My body stung as if it were on fire, then it stopped. There was nothing: no voices, no cold, no breathing. I was pulled from the icy water, there was no gasping. I saw Dr. Tarri's smile before my eyes rolled back into my head.

* * *

Yes, the cold is a peaceful way to die, but even on a winter's day like today, the chill couldn't compare to the isolation of freezing water. Today, there was just enough sting in the air to enjoy it.

The wind whipped around the boxwoods imitating the sounds of animals wrestling in the hedges. I half expected some stray cat to leap from the boxwoods and join my sister and me for tea. There was plenty of cream left and the grounds used to be sprawling with cats, but that was a long time ago.

Athena, seeing that my teacup was empty, refilled it. I studied her as she poured my tea. Sissy didn't notice, she was busy scribbling out her frustrations in her little notebook.

Seeing Athena outside of my bedroom always gave me a bit of a shock. She looked so different with her long hair tied up in a bun, a white bonnet covering her blonde curls—just as her dress blanketed her beautiful form. I much preferred how she looked naked. I wondered how she would look amongst the boxwoods unclothed—free. I imagined she'd look like a faerie of the Wild Hunt and I longed to join her there.

Sissy put down her book, closing it with a clap.

My eyes left Athena. I picked up my tea to take a sip primarily to hide my smile, my mind still on wild faeries. Athena placed a few finger sandwiches on my sister's plate and took the seat next to her. I thought this was brazen as Sissy didn't invite her to sit, but Sissy didn't seem to mind. She liked Athena as much as I did.

"I was thinking Ken," Sissy said with her mouth full. "We need to get you something special to wear for our birthday."

I looked down at myself. I was exceptionally dressed with the best finery my family fortune could afford. All of my wardrobe was new and had been waiting in my closet for me upon my return home. A few things didn't fit just right, but the tailor had taken care of that my first week home.

I did, however, make it a point not to wear anything around my neck, though a beautiful collection of cravats had been secured for me. I left the first few buttons on my dress shirt unfastened, allowing for a plunging neckline. I wanted to show off my collar bone, a quality I so admired in my sister.

"Don't get self-conscious Ken. You look great. Athena and I picked out every stitch of clothing you're wearing. I was just thinking it would be fun for us to get to pick things out together. We only turn eighteen once, let's make it special. I was thinking we have a masquerade themed birthday party."

"Masquerade themed sounds fine, but Father will never let me go into town. He said so himself. Not until I'm of age."

The thought of not leaving Dahl House until I was twenty-one did not bother me as it seemed to bother Sissy. I had everything I needed here. I had her.

Sissy understood me and loved me in a way no one else could. Maybe it came with the territory of being a twin, but I always knew it was more. There was and is nothing more important to me than our connection, this mingling of souls. It was what I was missing in the sanitarium and the need for it was the one thing that kept me going. Sissy was more than a lifeline; she was my life. And then there was Athena Elle Lee. Though she was still far from understanding me, there was real love there. I felt it in my chest every time I saw her—this laborious constriction, I had no control over. And I heard it in her heart at night when I rested by head on her bosom. Her heartbeat quickened the closer I was to her. Sometimes, I feared it would stop if it beat any faster. It was undeniable, we were in love. But could that be enough for me. Love without understanding. Was that even possible? Athena said she didn't want to replace Sissy, but could she? Could she, in fact, be Sissy's replacement? Again, this nagging feeling clawed at me from the inside of my skull. It felt like a hundred rats were trapped in there, their dagger-like claws scooping out my brain—Sissy wanted to leave Dahl house and I couldn't. I was trapped here. I had no allowance, no money of my own. I couldn't leave, but she could, and I feared she would leave me like Pluto had.

Not guessing at my inner turmoil, a smile danced across Sissy's face. "I already talked to Father, and he's agreed. We are to go to Madame Prospera's Boutique tomorrow night after the session with the portraitist. We're going after the store closes for private shopping. It will just be the two of us and we can stay as long as we like."

My eyes glossed over, a film of tears blurring my vision. I was not entirely sure why this gesture, on my sister's part, meant so much to me. I suppose I took it as a sign she wouldn't leave me behind.

"Shouldn't we visit Madame Prospera's before we are immortalized in paint?" I asked as the wind dried my wet eyes.

"Perhaps, but the painter is coming tomorrow to finish Father's portrait. We are merely an afterthought. But our portraits are from the neck up, so it doesn't make a lick of difference."

"There you are," a voice sounded behind me. Athena shot up.

I turned to see a face I hadn't seen since my early boyhood. Though only a few weeks my senior, his hairline had crawled back, and his nose was sharpened to a point, but I could never mistake those violet-tinted, melancholy eyes. They had this mystical quality about them that allowed these mystic orbs to pull the color from their surroundings, sending them into perpetual states of waxing and waning like two purple moons—it was the best friend of my boyhood—it was Eddy Poe.

He shook my gloved hand, seizing it with both of his. His grip was always firmer than mine and he shook my hand as if he expected to never see me again. "Glad to see you're doing well, Ken."

I was not pleased to see him, but I was not a rude man. I tilted my head toward my sister and Athena. "You remember—"

"Oh yes," he said, cutting me off and curtsying at my sister with the bend of one knee and a sweeping motion of his hat. "It's this lovely woman who wrote to me of your arrival. After my last visit, I told her to inform me the moment you came home, and we have been corresponding ever since."

I glanced at my sister incredulously. I didn't like the idea of anyone penning about me. Penning childhood fantasies were one thing, writing letters on the status of my wellbeing, something entirely different and inappropriate. We were no longer bosom friends, to the contrary, Eddy A. Poe was and is the closest thing I have to an enemy. I realized then that my being sent to Westminster and my time away had no ill effect on Sissy's and Eddy's relationship. If anything, it seemed to have strengthened it. He said he came because of her letter, but I was sure I was not the Dahl he was there to see.

It was true, Eddy and I were once very good friends but that was the past. I wanted nothing to do with him. He had already separated me from my sister once and I would not let him do it again. Maybe that had been his plan all along—get me out of the way, so he could have Sissy all to himself.

I could feel my cheeks flush. I hoped their already pinken glow brought on by the wind would mask my anger. I didn't need a scene. "I'm afraid you caught us at a bad time ole' boy. We have somewhere to be."

"That's a shame." He ran his gloved hand down the lapel of his coat.

"That *is* a shame," I said with a mock smile.

"I would like to talk to you about what happened. I desperately want to clear the air."

I nodded in the direction of Athena.

Understanding, he refrained.

I locked arms with Sissy. "I must bid you adieu, Edgar."

He bowed his head, again taking off his hat.

"I will check-in on you again. Kenneth . . . I've never stopped caring about you. You're always in my thoughts."

"That is kind of you, but I no longer need your pity."

My sister and I left through the hedge maze without another word. I glanced back at him where he stood with Athena. He was too close to her, I wished I could have whisked her away too.

"You don't like him," Sissy said accusingly.

"No, I don't, and you shouldn't either."

"You can't blame him for telling Father about the cats. Eventually, someone would have seen what you were doing and told him."

"Of course I can blame him. He was spying on me."

"Spying on you?" she laughed. I always loved her laugh. It sounded like high-pitched hiccups strung together. "Oh, darling Kenneth, he wasn't spying on you. He was coming to see me and just spied the wrong dark-haired angel."

"It's not funny Sissy. He's the reason we were separated."

"I'm not laughing at you, Ken."

I stopped. We stood alongside the silvery lake that kept its iridescent glow even without the aid of the moon. The few leaves left in the trees chattered in the wind keeping tune with our own chattering teeth. "Eddy and I have one thing in common. I want to clear the air about what happened. Seeing as you weren't there, and God only knows what you heard."

"Ken, I don't want to talk about it."

"But I do, and you need to hear this. I never killed one of those cats. None of them besides poor Pluto. But that was a horrible accident. You know how much I loved that cat. He followed me everywhere. We were seldom apart. For a while it was the three of us. I just hugged him too tightly, that's all. I didn't mean to asphyxiate him. My act was an act of love, not malice. Believe me, when I saw I killed him, I sobbed and I sobbed until my eyes were raw from what I'd done in the name of love—this love, this all-encompassing love, that I have only ever felt in his presence and yours."

Her hand tenderly moved across mine.

"I wanted to understand what made Pluto love me. That cat loved me like few things have in this world and I wanted to know what made Pluto different—what made him special. I thought if I took a closer look, I could understand it all, maybe even find a way to make others love me as he did and as you do.

"That's why I did it. That's why I opened him up—to see—to learn. It was in the name of science. But I quickly realized I required more specimens, so I could compare my findings. Sissy, what I was doing was science, not lunacy. I was keeping a detailed record of my discoveries. I was on the verge of understanding it all when Eddy followed me into my lab and told father what he saw."

She squeezed my hand.

This only acted to infuriate me. I didn't want her pity any more than I wanted Eddy's. My manner became excitable. "What I was doing was real science. Not that crackpot magic the doctors at Westminster call cutting-edge medicine. I was making real scientific advancements, and I wasn't hurting anyone. No—not like they hurt me. I wasn't doing that."

She held both of my hands now and stood in front of me, her shadow falling on the lake as the sun moved to set. "What about the voices honey? I thought they told you what to do?"

I shook my head, my nose pushing steam through my nostrils like a bated dragon. "No. That's not true. The voices merely suggested I take a look inside Pluto, and I thought that seemed very logical. I was in control. They didn't make me do anything. I decided with the freewill given to me by the heavenly Father to dissect him."

"But honey, there were no voices."

I pulled my hands free, folding them across my chest like a defiant child and turned from her. I took a deep breath to regain control and turned back in her direction, my arms falling to my side in a natural pose. "You're right," I said in a measured tone, "there were no voices."

"So, the doctors did help you?"

"Yes," I said through gritted teeth, not wanting to give them an ounce of credit because they deserved none.

I was in full control again. "I just wanted you to know why I did what I did. I noticed how jumpy everyone is, including you, when I pick up something sharp. I saw it in your eyes yesterday when I was helping Athena in the solarium with the pruning shears. I'm not going to just lose my head and stab someone."

"I know Kenneth."

"Trust me Sissy, I am harmless, and I have paid for my curiosity over and over again during the last four years."

CHAPTER TWELVE

Acute Senses

I filled the soaker tub in my private bathroom. I hadn't used the tub since my return home. I preferred showers to baths now and frequently used the basin on the washstand for convenience. It is curious how I went to the sanitarium fearing only that I would never see Sissy, to now fearing a number of silly things. In their attempt to fix me, who was not broken, they inevitably did break me, giving rise to trivial worries.

I feared water now. It seemed the most unnatural of all predilections. Water has always symbolized purity and cleansing and since the very first civilization, it has not only symbolized, but has given rise to life. Water comes from the sky. It is natural. It is good, like the cold. To fear it is like fearing the very heavens.

It's true, I did not fear it in the sense that I could not be near it or shrank from it when I saw it. Taking in the view of the tarn, lakeside or through my bedroom window, seeing its shimmering surface was a favorite pastime of mine. Water, as always, has remained a source of intrinsic beauty to me. I feared the idea of being submerged in it, not drowning. No, that wasn't it. I had almost been drowned and found it to be a more peaceful way to die, preferred to death via pain or any other mode Westminster had to offer. I feared the isolation of my body and mind that came from being submerged. Feared my senses being muffled. Feared the very sensation of touch smothered in liquid gloves. For, through this shutting out, it was only natural for other things to be amplified.

I let the tub fill with hot water. I was performing my own little experiment today. I was going to prove to myself I could overcome anything Dr. Tarri did to me. I could and will overcome any obstacle. The inconvenience of Eddy's visit, the fear of losing Sissy again, the fear of taking a simple bath, were all obstacles to overcome. I will take a bath without consequence and be better for it. Who knows, maybe I would again favorite them over the wash basin. Then, I would move on to my next roadblock.

The bathroom filled with steam, coating the windows in a film of condensation. It made me feel like I was trapped in a cloud. The air becoming heavy, moisture dampened my hair and clothes. I let my fingertips sit in the water as I leaned over the filling tub. Was it being submerged in this tub I feared or was it death? I laughed. It was a quick burst of sound that was lost in the piping steam. To fear death was the silliest thing of all. Death is not absolute but infinite; I was and am sure about that. I had heard the voices of the fallen clearer than my own voice.

Though I consider myself a man of science, there was the science of the stars and sky—the science of the gods, we as mere mortals cannot understand. The Egyptians knew this. They spent their entire lives preparing for the life after—the afterlife. The knowledge was lost over time and replaced with new gods—Titans like Helios replaced Horus, then more gods, and ultimately a God. But as Dr. Tarri always said, 'perception does not change the empirical truth'. That being, death is not finite. There is no reason to fear it and I would prove that to myself now.

I took my time undressing. I was no longer cold. The steam laden room had already thawed the numbness left in my chin and nose from the chill of lunching in the hedge garden. Running my hand over the condensation on the bathroom window, I could see the most eastern part of the lake and the entrance into the gardens. Eddy stood in front of the entrance, a black smear amongst the boxwoods; he was still with Athena. My chest tightened at seeing him even from this distance. He had taken so much from me. I had trusted him, and he had taken from me.

He looked like an insect, a little black ant on my window. It would be so easy to crush him under my fist. I longed to take from him like he took from me. Death is too good for him. Too quick a punishment. He should be made to suffer like I was made to.

I finished undressing and went to the tub. I dipped my hand into the water to only withdraw it. The water was hot—too hot. But that's how I wanted it. The last time I was in a tub the water was freezing, this would give balance to the old memories bouncing around in my head and bring clarity.

I stepped into the copper tub. I stood there for a few minutes, allowing my body a chance to adjust to the temperature, before sitting down. The last time I was in my tub, I fit better. My growth spurt made it necessary for my knees to remain folded into my chest to fit. I felt like a cat who has pressed themselves into a box half their size. But much how a cat must feel, I felt safe and secure. Yes, I was not afraid of this or death. I relaxed, resting my head back, letting the heat penetrate me as I let the cold once.

* * *

"You scared me today, Ken."

"How so?" I asked, tracing the button of Dr. Tarri's couch cushion.

"You don't remember."

In thought, I looked to the ceiling. I don't think I had ever done that before. The ceiling was yellow from smoke. It was the closest thing I had to a sun while committed. It disgusted me that the sun was in Dr. Tarri's office. I looked to my captor. "I remember the cold and your face . . . I think I will always remember your face."

"You fainted. I thought for a second, I'd killed you."

I ran my tongue over my teeth in thought. "Have you killed a patient before?"

With a curt, sharp tone he said, "Ken, you're not a colleague, you don't get to ask me those sorts of questions."

Without feeling, for I didn't care that my question flustered him, I remarked, "I am well aware I am a patient, and you are a doctor. You don't have to try to make me feel smaller than I am. You could have just said yes."

Dr. Tarri sat next to me on the couch. "I'm sorry. I really thought I had killed you. I'm still a little on edge. For now on, we will stick to pain to manage your symptoms. Isolation doesn't work for you."

"But it did. I felt nothing and heard nothing."

"That's because you almost died."

"Is that what it's like to die, then? That peaceful calm. I don't fear that, and neither should you."

"I do Kenneth, all sane men do. Even the most pious man fears death. Fears judgment from God."

"I wonder if they fear the right god."

"What god do you fear, Ken?" he asked in the tone he reserved for lessons.

"If I answer wrong, will I be punished?"

"This is not as session. It's just us talking."

He nodded as if to give me his word.

Westminster was prison for all walks of life, from the educated like myself, to street urchins. Sometimes Dr. Tarri just wanted to talk. I knew my place. I was the suppressed, he was the suppressor. He'd want to talk candidly, like we were bosom friends, just chatting about philosophy or the arts. Sometimes he wanted to talk as lovers, sharing special little things not to be shared with others. On the latter occasion, I would just listen. I listened to everything he said, filing it away, learning from it.

"I don't fear a god, Dr. Tarri. I fear being separated from the ones I love. This asylum has become a hell for me. It keeps me from where I want to be. I'm living my greatest fear. The sanitarium has made me fear other things that are trivial, oh so trivial to that one thing—going home. I don't want to die here, Dr. Tarri. I want to return home. I want to see my sister."

He rubbed the top of his hand. "But you can't Ken, because everyone there fears you."

My voice cracked, I momentarily lost control. "That's fantastical nonsense!"

"It's not. That's why you're here. Your family fears for you and fears you." He was back to using his clinic voice. "I hope you were exaggerating when you called this place a hell."

I looked at him with cool eyes, restraint evident in my tone. "I am not one for exaggerations of heart or spirit."

"Let's try something."

"I thought you said this wasn't a session."

"It's not. I just want to try something." He untied his cravat.

It was dark gray, almost black. It may have been black a long time ago. "Tie this around your eyes."

Taking the cravat, I did what he said. There was no point in refusing him. He had all the power. The material was warm against my eyelids. I could smell his aftershave. It had a minty scent.

"The ice water was meant to put your entire body in a state of isolation. Let's try targeting your vision. Sight is how you primarily take things in. But what if you were blind. How would you perceive things?"

I pulled the wrap from my eyes to ascertain his intentions. "Wouldn't wearing a blindfold, make my other senses more acute. Wouldn't my hearing, my sense of touch, my sense of smell be made sharper by the loss of my vision?"

Dr. Tarri got up. Going to the lamp, he turned it off. "It's true you hear the voices, but you rely on your sight to perceive them more than your ears. I've seen it so many times now. Your eyes ping every time you hear one. Remember—*believe nothing you hear, and only one half that you see.*"

Returning to the couch, he pulled the cravat back over my eyelids. "Tell me Ken, what do you feel, having your eyes closed, while you're awake? What do you perceive?"

"I perceive nothing. I feel nothing in particular. I am awake with my eyes closed staring at the inside of my eyelids."

A shadow drifted in front of my closed eyes. I could make out grooves—scratches. Everything was dark, too dark. No light penetrated my blindfold. I heard a light grating noise. It grew louder—louder. The sound traveled from my ears into my head. Yes, the scratching was in my skull now. It tore at my brain.

"What is it?" Dr. Tarri asked, seeing me shift into agitation.

"The scratching is in my head! It's clawing at me! Help me!" The grating noise had grown to a hideous pitch. "It hurts!"

"Ken, nothing is hurting you. You're sitting with me on the couch in my office. Try to relax, remember what you've learned. Your emotions give your psychosis power. Turn them off."

"I smell smoke."

"I'm not smoking," Dr. Tarri said.

"It's hard to breathe. It keeps getting louder. Make it stop. Please, make it stop. I can't stand the noise!" I dragged my nails down the sides of my face, scratching my ears and cheeks.

He grabbed my wrists, stopping my next assault.

Tears gushed from my closed eyes. "Please, help me."

He pulled the blindfold from my eyes, my eyes flashing wide-open. I felt the sting of the scratches on my face and the hot tears on my cheeks. I lost control. My pulse hiccupped. "I'm sorry," I said in a whisper, fearing punishment. "I'm so sorry, Dr. Tarri."

He pressed the cravat to the side of my face to catch the blood, then to the other side to do the same.

"Please don't hurt me," I said. My voice quaked. My throat was dry as if I had been yelling. I could scarcely make out Dr. Tarri's face in the dim room, but I thought I saw fear in his coal-like eyes.

He wrapped his arms around me, drawing me so close to him it was hard to breathe. The heat of his body acted to smother me. I wanted to claw myself free, but he held me in place sensing this struggle within me. "I'm sorry Kenneth. I knew it. I knew isolation techniques are not good for you. Depriving you of your senses makes it worse. Never again Ken. Never deprive your senses. Promise me you won't."

* * *

I opened my eyes to Athena. To the blue sky of her eyes. To the golden sun that is her hair. She was crying, her arms were thrown around me.

"Athena? . . ." I said, my hand going to her silken hair. She

83

smelled of the sun. She smelled of me. She orbited around me, her god of the sun—her Helios. The gods of old have seized the day.

"I thought you were dead. I came to tell you dinner was being served at the top of the hour, to find you in your tub."

I glanced around my lavatory. It was true, it was late. The sun had set; the bathroom was bathed in shadows. The water was no longer hot, but cool.

My finger traced her tears. "I must have fallen asleep."

"Please don't frighten me like that again."

"I won't, I promise. That's two times now I've frightened you. There will not be a third. Hand me a towel?"

I stood, taking the towel from Athena. I wrapped it around her. "Your soaked. You'll catch a cold." The sleeves of her dress were drenched. I wasn't sure if it was the scare or her wet dress that had her shaking like a leaf. I pressed her to me, her warmth my own towel.

"I knew you were upset about Eddy stopping by and I thought . . ."

"You thought what? . . . That I ended my life because of him." I lifted her chin. "He took my life from me once, and I will not let him do it again. I have returned home to have more than I ever had. I am sure it is more than he *has*. I am the lucky man. It is he who should be pitied."

"You mean that?" she asked with an earnest smile.

With my thumbs, I wiped the tears beading on her thick lashes. "Yes."

She pressed her lips to mine. They were so warm and filled with life. Yes, this little flower of a girl gave me life. This little violet. I helped her slip out of her wet dress. I wrapped a towel around the both of us. The sum of our bodies produced a sun-like heat that could penetrate through the densest of strangling vines. Athena was so soft in my arms. So lovely. This is what I feared. I feared being separated from the ones I love—not water, not pain, not death, but separation. I had escaped Hell and now enjoyed paradise.

CHAPTER THIRTEEN

The Hidden Meaning of Things

I entered my room to find Athena leaning on the small table next to my chair reading by lamp light. Her face was flush with color, her eyes looked like passing clouds as she scanned her book. I had been in the cellar longer than usual, losing track of the time in the mirror.

"I hope I haven't kept you waiting."

"Not at all. I have a new book I'm reading, it's wonderful."

I took a seat in my armchair. She tilted the book in my direction for me to see the cover.

"*The Hidden World of Flowers,*" I read.

"Yes, it tells you the meaning behind every flower."

"Ah, yes, for instance the violet symbolizes wisdom, like the mighty Pallas Athena whom you were named for. Let's not forget the violet is also symbolic of loyalty and faithfulness. Yes, the violet is the flower that reminds me of you most. As my violet, I know you will never leave me. You will always be with me."

Her eyes lit up, looking very much like a violet, her blue eyes pulling purple from my curtains.

"How romantic. What flower are you?"

"Um . . . I'm not sure. I guess a marigold. In some cultures the marigold represents the sun. You're Athena, so I'm Helios."

She turned to the 'M's, finding marigold. "'The sun's ray or light leading the departed to heaven' . . . that sounds a bit morbid. I don't know if I like that."

I chuckled. "It does when it's worded like that. Try daisy, that's my favorite flower."

She turned to the page. "Daisies are symbolic of innocence, loyal love, and purity." She grinned, reading on. "If you gift a daisy to a friend, that means you won't tell anyone their secret."

She stared at me, excitably. "Oh yes Ken, you're a daisy. I gave you a daisy on your first morning home. I placed it on the side of your breakfast tray. Do you remember?"

"I do."

"I had no idea it meant that."

I smiled, thinking of the daisy wallpaper I'd just come from. The daisy, with its yellow sun-like core and its small white petals that wrap around its center protectively, has its own mask. Yes, daisies suit me.

"We have it then. I am a daisy and you are a violet. Let's see," I said, tapping on my chin, "Sissy would be a morning glory. Few flowers open and close every day for the sun. That's how I view her. In my presence she opens up, just like the morning glory at dawn."

"Yes, I think that's right too," she said. "You know so much about flowers. I think you know more than me."

I shook my head good-humoredly. "Not possible. You know how to tend them. You like making them grow, I just like looking at them. Understanding the secret meaning behind things has always interested me. And I only know what I do because I've read that book many times."

Athena's eyebrows arched to peaks. "You have?"

"Yes. It was one of my favorites in my boyhood. That book belonged to my mother, and I claimed it for myself. I wouldn't even let Sissy borrow it."

"Oh," she said, looking down at the tan linen cover as if knowing it had belonged to me in the past had changed it in the present.

"If you turn to the last page, you'll see my name written at the bottom."

She turned the book to the last page, running her finger over my name: Kenneth Live Dahl.

"I'm sorry. I had no idea it was your mother's or yours. Your father gave it to me."

"He was right to give it to you. My mother is dead and as I am forbidden to read, I'm glad it found its way into your hands."

I took her hand and pressed a kiss to the back of it, meaning my words and my kiss.

"That's a silly rule."

"Yes, well, my father is a silly man. No mirrors and no books. I suppose he worries that the books will fill my head with the nonsense of my youth."

"There's no harm in reading books about flowers."

I pressed another kiss to her hand. "There mustn't be, or you wouldn't let me read the ones in the solarium. My goddess of wisdom and war would never allow harm to come to me."

"It's just a book about flowers," she said as if she was worried the books *could* harm me. "They just teach you how to prune properly."

"Yes, on the surface that's all. It's the hidden meanings I take from books that worry him." I stood. "Enough about my father. If you're going to be the caretaker of those innocent books, I would like you to take better care of them." I pointed to the page corner she had folded over.

"Sorry," she said, "I was using a ribbon for a bookmark, but it keeps slipping out."

"I've noticed and that's why I made you this." I went to my bureau and opened the top drawer, pulling out a bookmarker. Her name ran down the middle in blue embroidery with purple violets interconnecting to make the border. I handed it to her. "For you, Athena."

She examined it under the lamp light. "Ken, you made this? It's beautiful. It has my flower. The violets are perfect."

"Yes," I said, returning to my chair. "I learned to embroider when I was very young. My grandmother always had poor eyesight and she needed help with the more complex stitches. Sissy had no interest in it, but I liked making things, so my grandmother taught me."

Athena held it to her bosom. "Thank you."

"While Sissy's been working on her writing, I've been working on your bookmark. I just finished it today. It's amazing I got it done after Eddy showed up out of the blue."

Ignoring my comment about Eddy she proudly asserted, "You see a problem and you fix it. This reminds me of one of my favorite stories Sissy wrote about you."

"You can't believe everything she writes. I think I make more problems than I fix."

"I know this story is true."

"Pray tell, what story would that be?"

"The one when you fixed her porcelain doll."

I laughed, my laugh came out in hiccups, sounding a lot like Sissy's. "Oh, that story is very true. Sissy broke her favorite doll. She carried that doll around with her everywhere. It was custom made to look like her. It had her beautiful face with her two different colored eyes and her dark hair and her full lips. She loved that doll so much that when she dropped it and its face shattered, she was inconsolable. Father refused to get her another one. It was his way of teaching her to take better care of her things. I couldn't stand to see her cry. So, I took the doll out of the trash along with as many pieces to its face as I could find. I glued the doll back together but there were a lot of pieces missing."

"That's when you broke all of the dishes."

"Yes, it just so happened our finest china matched the color of her doll's face. I broke every single dish looking for the perfect shaped piece to fill in the missing pieces in the doll's face." I grinned. "Who knew making my own puzzle pieces would be so labor intensive or expensive. My father was so angry. I wish you could've seen him. He was as red as a lobster. If it weren't for my grandmother, I think he would have murdered me that day. I remember saying to him the dishes aren't lost Father, they just live in Sissy's doll now."

Athena laughed into her bookmark. "You have a heart of gold Ken."

"I don't know if I'd agree with that. I just couldn't stand to see Sissy so upset and since my father wouldn't get her a new doll, he left me very little choice. Sissy's happiness is worth more than the cost of the dishes."

She sat on my lap wrapping her arms around my neck, her bookmark still in her hands. "Yep, like I said, you see a problem and you fix it. You truly are the sweetest man, and it's for thinking like that, I love you."

I blushed, after months of intimacy she could still do that to me.

"She has the doll still, you know? It's in her room."

"I've seen it. That's how I knew the story was true. You did a good job repairing it."

I laughed. "Not bad for an eight-year-old. Well, shall I read to you tonight and blatantly disobey my father yet again?"

"That would be lovely," she said, resting her head against my shoulder, her arms still wrapped in a warm embrace around my neck. "I love it when you read to me."

I reached for the book she left on the table. "Where did you leave off or should I look for a folded page?"

She kissed the side of my cheek. "Don't be cheeky Ken. I'm on rampion."

I pressed a kiss to her eye. And what eyes they were. Even closed they seemed to sparkle like stars. "Oh yes rampion, a member of the bellflower family."

* * *

While I waited for Dr. Tarri to get dressed, I scanned his bookcase. The walnut bookcase spanned two walls forming a sharp corner of the room. On it were ancient books and curious tomes. Many medical books, I dare not say all, I assumed were his when he was a schoolboy. They appeared as old and tidy as he was. I would have been interested in these medical books, if my current predicament was different, but I couldn't bear to open them and see what agonies awaited me. Instead, I focused on a singular shelf that housed books of poetry, philosophy, and to my relish—children's stories. I was no longer a child, but on this particular day I couldn't resist pulling out a binding of *Grimm's Fairy Tales*. I would have done anything to return to the days of Sissy and me leisurely reading together—doing anything together.

Dr. Tarri's sharp eyes watched me like a hawk as he dressed. He had not given me permission, something I explicitly needed in all matters. In explanation I told him, "Rapunzel was my favorite story as a boy."

"Why's that?" he asked, tucking in his shirt.

"I always liked that Rapunzel's mother ate a diet of rampion when she was pregnant with her. I liked the irony of her mother giving birth to a child nourished solely on rampion to be named after the flower and who later blooms into a beautiful flower of a girl. Then this beautiful girl is locked away from everyone and everything where no one can enjoy her beauty."

"Are you Rapunzel in the story?"

"No."

"So, you're not the victim . . ." Dr. Tarri said, thoughtfully. "The handsome prince then? Perhaps, you see yourself as the hero to your own story?"

I opened the book, looking at the illustrations of the beautiful Rapunzel, her long hair coiled around her like a rope. "The handsome prince discovers Rapunzel because he hears her singing, much like how we would discover a flower by smell. He watches the evil enchantress call for Rapunzel to throw down her hair so she can climb up the tower through its only window. The prince learns the secret of Rapunzel and how to get into the tower. Before he climbs her hair, he picks a rose from the rosebush that surrounds the tower as a gift for his love. He does this every day after the evil enchantress leaves."

I glanced to Dr. Tarri, who was busy adjusting his waistcoat. He had missed a button and had to start over. "No, I'm not the prince or Rapunzel. Rapunzel is my sister locked away at Dahl

House and my childhood friend, Eddy, is the prince. Your so-called hero of the story."

"You're the wicked enchantress then? You see yourself as the villain?"

"No, that privilege goes to my father."

He studied me. I went on with the story as if he was not familiar with it. "The evil enchantress learns of the prince's visits and cuts Rapunzel's hair, setting a trap for him. When the prince climbs up Rapunzel's hair, expecting to see his love, to find the old witch waiting for him, the witch releases the rope of hair, and he falls from the tower into the rosebush." I closed the book, my eyes locked on Dr. Tarri. "Dr. Tarri, I'm the rosebush. The one whose thorns pierce the prince's eyes and blind him." I slid the book back in its place on the shelf. "Yes, I'm the unassuming rosebush."

"I see that," he said in a whisper. "Beautiful, yet deadly."

"A red rose symbolizes love, but no one talks about the meaning behind the thorns."

"What does that mean to you, Kenneth?"

"The thorn is symbolic of sin and hardship. The rose is the living embodiment of pain and pleasure. What a pity a rosebush has more thorns than flowers."

CHAPTER FOURTEEN

Demon in My View

I stood next to Athena in the sitting room as the painter put the finishing touches on my father's portrait. I seldom came into this room, though it had a nice view of the lake through the many windows facing the front of the house. It also had a comprehensive view of Dahl Cemetery and the lone Poplar tree that arched over it like the hands of the grim reaper. I found something about the duplicity of the view comforting and unsettling as if through these windows I could see life and death—see the living and the dead as if they were one. It just so happened that the tarn lined up with my dark-brown eye and the cemetery aligned with my pale-blue one.

The room itself was furnished with a seating group next to the hearth where a fire blazed. Also, there was a large desk and piano in the room, along with numerous vases filled with fresh flowers that stood on small tables wherever there seemed to be space until the room was quite full. The sitting room should have been a comfortable space if the dull drudgery of the dining hall didn't pervade every inch of the room, mind the fresh flowers.

The crackling and popping of the fire were the only sounds in the room besides my father's heavy breathing. I believed this habit was developed for pomp rather than it being a consequence of him being overweight. He rather relished people taking notice of him for one reason or another.

My father stood next to the hearth with one elbow on the mantle, the other holding his walking cane, a raspy hiss leaving his lips every third exhale.

"He holds his cane like it's a king's scepter," Athena whispered to me.

The corners of my lips curled upward. "Are you making fun of my father Athena?"

"A little," she said with a smirk.

"I can see the resemblance to King Henry the VIII."

She bit back a giggle. I loved it when she did that. This strive for self-control, this vulnerability, made her more beautiful to me. Despite her perfect form, her perfect eyes, she was inevitably flawed like me. My hand reached for hers, knowing I couldn't hold it, I let my fingertips graze her hand. I longed for the day I could do what I wanted. If I wanted to hold her hand, I *could* hold it. But I had a tyrant in my way. Sissy was right, we were an afterthought. My father stood in his best suit with his walking cane and hat tucked under the nook of his elbow like it was a crown.

Sissy, accompanied by my grandmother, entered the sitting room wearing a blood-red gown, instantly giving life to the room. They forked, my grandmother going to the painter's side and Sissy coming to mine. Cracking a smile I said, "I thought he was only painting us from the head up?"

Not that that would have changed my attire much. I already had a violet in my buttonhole given to me by Athena, but maybe I would have requested something in red to accompany the violet to match Sissy or sought out a morning glory.

"The poor painter has to look at us for hours on end, I thought I would give him something nice to look at."

And she did. There were few colors that did not suit Sissy. Red was a natural complement to her dark hair and fair complexion. Where the bold color would have washed out other girls, it made her look like a queen. The high collar of the dress came to her chin, her face a rosebud.

"That's very thoughtful of you Sissy. And it looks like you're right on time."

The painter stood, beckoning my father to look at the portrait. My grandmother was pleased, offering the painter her congratulations on a job well done. My father sauntered over. He looked at his portrait for quite some time, moving his head up and down in exaggerated motions, before shaking the painter's hand.

It was our turn. Athena dragged over a chair for me to sit in. I sat, resting my hands on the padded arm rests. Although my portrait was being painted first, Sissy stood next to me as if we were being painted together. I liked that idea more but didn't suggest it to my father. That was exactly the kind of suggestion he would take as disrespect, especially if asked in front of the painter.

Following the painter's instruction, I turned my head slightly toward him.

"Perfect Mr. Dahl," he said in a thick accent. "Mucho perfection. Bella!"

The painter went to work immediately. I tried to remain as still as possible, directing my attention on Athena. My father took my place by her side, while my grandmother took a seat opposite the fire. I wished I could make out what he was whispering to her. My eyes flashed toward the door. It was Eddy Poe accompanied by the doorman. He had said he would be checking in on me. I didn't think he meant the next day.

I remained calm, unmoved. I had no choice, the painter demanded it of me, and my father was in the room. Eddy shook my father's hand, spending a great deal of time saying hello to Athena before making his way over to me.

"This looks like fun," he said, standing opposite Sissy. My head was positioned away from him, no doubt he chose that position to take advantage of my blindness. It was just like him to take advantage of a situation. But yet, I preferred him where he stood; away from my beloved sister.

"Loads."

"Athena told me you were having your portrait painted today and I thought I should stop by. I know how tiresome the whole process can be."

"I'm quite alright. I like tiresome. *Leave my loneliness unbroken.*"

Ignoring my request he said, "I thought maybe I can entertain you with a little poetry while you wait."

"Yes please," Sissy said, her eyes lighting up.

"That's not necessary."

"Oh Kenneth," Sissy whined.

"Fine, one poem, and make it a short one."

He pulled out a little notebook that rivaled Sissy's. I was sure if she was getting a full body portrait, she would want to be painted with her notebook. Maybe that's why she wore red. It was symbolic of that little red notebook of hers. After all, the violet in my buttonhole was symbolic of Athena, violets signifying wisdom, loyalty, and faithfulness. Athena is and would always be *my* goddess—my very own Pallas Athena.

Eddy stopped thumbing through his book. "Here it is. I haven't titled this poem yet. I'm not sure if I ever will or if I will pursue publication, but I originally penned it four years ago and think it's worth you hearing."

"That's some introduction, Eddy . . . A juvenilia poem that you have not bothered to title and don't feel is good enough for publication. Well, if that's your choice, then get on with it."

Without further ado he began. His violet eyes reading each word with a wisdom greater than he.

> *"From childhood's hour I have not been*
> *As others were -- I have not seen*
> *As others saw -- I could not bring*
> *My passions from a common spring --*
> *From the same source I have not taken*
> *My sorrow -- I could not awaken*
> *My heart to joy at the same tone --*
> *And all I lov'd -- I lov'd alone --*
> *Then -- in my childhood -- in the dawn*
> *Of a most stormy life -- was drawn*
> *From ev'ry depth of good and ill*
> *The mystery which binds me still --*
> *From the torrent, or the fountain --*
> *From the red cliff of the mountain --*
> *From the sun that 'round me roll'd*
> *In its autumn tint of gold --*
> *From the lightning in the sky*
> *As it pass'd me flying by --*
> *From the thunder, and the storm --*
> *And the cloud that took the form*
> *(When the rest of Heaven was blue)*
> *Of a demon in my view -"*

"Oh Eddy," Sissy gushed, her hands going to her bosom as if to stop her heart from falling out of her chest and landing on the painter's shoes. "That was so heartfelt. I love it!"

He looked to me.

"Yes—yes, very good," I said, looking at him out of the corner of my eye.

I could relate to his little poem. I too felt isolated. An isolation I first brought upon myself, and was later inflicted on me by others against my will. I was surprised to learn that Eddy felt that way too. Or is this nameless poem about me? He penned it four years ago. Was it about me being sent away to the sanitarium? Was it about Eddy realizing I, his best friend, was not as others were since the day of my birth. It was explicitly true; I had not seen as others saw. The mystery that binds us was no other than the day he followed me into the potting shed. The dawn of discovery was the moment he opened the potting shed door and glimpsed my inner demon. This poem was untitled because its title was my name: The Fall of the House of Dahl.

I glanced at Athena, hoping she didn't guess at the poem's hidden meaning. If this was Eddy's idea of an apology, it was he who deserved to be locked away at Westminster.

I gasped, jumping to my feet. Passing behind Athena was the faceless woman, her face darker in the light of the room, her white dress taking on the same bioluminescence it did in the catacombs.

"Athena behind you!" I shouted.

Everyone turned around.

"What's the matter with you?!" My father scolded, turning to see nothing out of the ordinary.

My grandmother adjusted her spectacles, looking behind her again.

I realized all too keenly, I was the only one who had seen the faceless woman. But not even I had glimpsed her for a long time. She vanished. She existed only for the few seconds it took her to pass behind Athena.

I had not thought the faceless woman to be maleficent when I first recalled her. Her voice, after all, I had assumed to be the voice of my mother's, making this phantom the spiritual embodiment of my beloved mother. But then I remembered the push on my shoulder and was not sure if the faceless woman was friend or foe. I doubted very much this woman was my mother now. My mother, I knew, would be wholly good. I would feel no opposition toward her.

I had not seen the faceless woman or heard any voices since the night I ventured into my family's underground crypt. There was not one peep, not one whisper. The house had been silent.

Seeing the faceless woman in broad daylight without provocation terrified me. The voices always seemed harmless. They were there for guidance. If I needed help, they imparted their wisdom to me. But to see an apparition that no one else could see, made me doubt my own senses—made me feel out of control. *Yet mad I am not . . . and very surely do I not dream.*

"Nothing's wrong with me," I said, my voice shaky. "I just need a glass of water from the pitcher behind Athena." There, that took care of it—behind Athena was the water pitcher.

Promptly, Athena brought me a glass of water. My hand trembled as I brought the glass to my lips. Athena and Sissy stood in front of me to block my father's view. Athena placed her hand over mine to ensure I didn't drop my glass.

"Are you okay?" she whispered to me, her large, blue eyes webbing over in red.

"Yes, I was just overcome with thirst."

Athena and Eddy exchanged worried looks.

"I should go," he said. He shook my hand. I didn't have the energy to put on a show for his benefit. My shake was listless.

CHAPTER FIFTEEN

Madame Prospera's Boutique

We arrived at Madame Prospera's Boutique at dusk. I watched people hurrying home down the street. I hadn't seen that many people all in one place since the sanitarium. I found it comical, almost to the point of crying, that whether trapped in a psychiatric hospital or free to roam the streets, people all scurried like rats.

My sister hopped out of the carriage, reaching her small hand back into its depths to take mine. I hesitated not, I was still a little shaky from the afternoon. I was surprised after my outburst our father didn't cancel with Madame Prospera. But I was glad he didn't. I would've hated for Sissy's plans to be laid to waste because I lost control.

I took Sissy's hand and alighted from the carriage onto the newly deserted street. Madame Prospera's Boutique faced the east and spanned one city block. The setting sun was already far behind the black and white striped awnings. My eyes danced over the mannequins in the store front window. The rich velvet of one dress seemed like liquid next to the lacy frock of its neighbor. And it all seemed like the perfect contrast to the brick exterior of Madame Prospera's.

A hand painted sign, denoting the exclusive clothing boutique, hung over the sidewalk in swirls of silver and gold tones. There was something about the sign that excited me. My sister and I had been out of the house so seldom as children, everyone from tailors, tutors, and toymakers always came to us. Visiting the playhouse with our grandmother as children was so faded now, I couldn't recall a single play we had seen. I had no clear-cut memory of what the outside world looked like and thus never missed it nor longed for it. But now I was filled with a burning excitement at experiencing something new.

While I continued to marvel at the store front, Sissy spoke to the coachman. It was the same driver who had taken me to Westminster and in turn delivered me home. He, as what had become expected, avoided my gaze, tucking his eyes under the wide brim of his hat.

"Stay with the coach," she ordered.

Returning to me, she took my hand, flashing a smile. Time may have changed me, but we still shared that same smile.

"Come on Ken, the good stuff's inside."

Before she could knock on the door it opened and we were greeted by a large, jovial woman in a black dress. Feathers of blue, purple, green, orange, white, black, and red jutted out from her lavish black hat like a rainbow peacock. I had never seen a woman like her before. Madame Prospera was almost as tall as me, which was tall even for a man, and she was as wide as the entrance. There was an energy about her that seemed frenzied and absurdly extravagant.

When she stepped inside to let us in, I was met with a flash of color as if the plumes in her hat unfolded the rainbow. My eyes didn't know where to focus, that was until she stepped back in front of me and my eyes went to her chins. I had never seen so many in one place. They fascinated me. They looked like lumpy steps leading down to her chest which was exposed in a way I was not accustomed to—more soft lumps.

"I beg your pardon," I said, my eyes darting back to her face. "I . . . I was . . . "

She seemed pleased that I noticed the voluminousness of her breasts. "Mr. Dahl, I'm so pleased to make your acquaintance." She put her gloved hand to my mouth for me to kiss, which I did with the ceremony deserving of such a unique woman. The black velvet felt like soft fur on my lips and recalled me to Pluto.

"My shop is yours tonight," she said, once I released her hand. "I do wish I was staying, it's not every day I have such a beautiful, young man in my shop."

The word man stung me, the pang hit me in the center of my heart like indigestion. I knew that's what I was, I had referred to myself that way, but I would prefer her to call me anything but that. The word didn't suit me. But to be referred to as beautiful, that was unexpected and nice. I wondered if she meant it or if she felt obliged to flatter all of her patrons.

"You have my boutique to yourself for as long as you like. I live above the shop, so if you need me for anything don't hesitate." Madame Prospera leaned in, thrusting her chest in my direction. "I'm just a ring away." On the wall was a bell, not unlike the ones hanging on the wall in the servant dining hall. When we pushed a button the coordinating bell would ring, alerting the servants where in the house we were to be found.

She pointed at a small, ornate table painted in an oriental style. On top of it sat a plate with a lovely spread of cheeses, crackers, and fruits. "In case you get peckish, I set out some treats, help yourself. When you've shopped your last, leave your selections on the cashier's desk and I will have them wrapped and sent to your house. If alterations are needed, we can do them here or I can come to you. And if you don't find what you're looking for, I can always design something custom." Twirling around as if she was dancing with an invisible partner, she continued. "Use what you see here as inspiration."

She really was a queer sort of creature. I instantly liked her. "Thank you, Madame Prospera. You're too kind."

She held her hand up for it to be kissed again, I complied readily, planting another kiss on the fur-like velvet. "Remember, I'm just a ring away."

"Where should we start?" Sissy asked, the moment Madame Prospera left us.

"I don't know," I said, taking it all in. There were racks upon racks of dresses, including: mourning dresses, day dresses, evening dresses, and ballgowns. Bonnets of every color imaginable hung from the walls like butterflies. I spied a small men's section in the corner. I walked over to it, thumbing through the waistcoats. The men's wear was very plain compared to the elaborate dresses and the superfluous abundance of choices for women. "Disappointing," I muttered. "Everything looks like the garments I already own."

"I have an idea," Sissy said, giggling into her palm.

I raised an eyebrow in her direction. "What's that?"

"We could play dress up like we did when we were children."

I smiled. "I was going to suggest the same thing." It was

incredible how she could seemingly read my mind. Oh yes, Sissy understood me—understood me like no one else could.

She grabbed my hand and rushed me over to a rack of ballgowns. "Look, they have your size!" She pulled out a black gown. It was made of the finest silk. The cut was off the shoulder, and it had an empire waist, flaring to the ground in a slight train. "This is the one! What do you think?"

I ran my hand down the material, it was as smooth as ice. "It's beautiful."

"They have it in both of our sizes. Let's try it on."

I quickly unbuttoned my waistcoat, almost sending a button flying. It held on by a cobweb of a string. It had been so long since I put on a dress. And now that I was grown, I thought I never would again. I tossed off my shirt. Leaving my pants in a heap on the ground, I stepped into the black gown. It fit me perfectly, the smooth material gliding effortlessly over my thighs and chest. I rushed out of the dressing room anxious to hear Sissy's thoughts. She had already slid on the dress and was waiting for me. She looked stunning. The neckline suited her as I hoped it did me, and the pinched waist accented her femininity.

"How do I look Sissy?"

"Gorgeous!"

I ran my hands down the dress. "I wish I could see myself." I longed for my mirror. I longed to see the black silk against my white skin—to see the draping neckline scoop under my collar bone.

She took my hand, pulling me along.

"Where are we going?"

She stopped in the back of the store. To the side of the door Madame Prospera took to go to her upstairs apartment, was a massive rectangular object blanketed by a throw. I knew at once it had to be a mirror.

My heart pounded, a nervous energy pulsing through my every fiber. "Pull it down Sissy." She did and there we stood together in front of Madame Prospera's mirror in matching dresses—with our matching black hair and our mismatched eyes. We were a sight. I took her hand.

I smiled at my reflection. I loved the dress. I loved how it exposed my neck and collar bone. The absence of breasts didn't take away from the pillowing neckline that hung off my shoulders, it made it all the more splendid. Time had taken away my gentle chin, but luckily did not give me a protruding Adam's apple like my father. My neck was as smooth and long as my sister's and this dress accented it perfectly. My neck was made to wear chokers not neckties.

Sissy turned to me, still holding my hand. "You always did look better in a dress than me."

"You're just saying that."

"No," she said, running her hand over her chest. "Even your chest looks better in the dress. I think it's because your broader than me." She poked my pectoral. It was firm and hard under the pressure of her finger, nothing like Madame Prospera's soft lumps.

Sissy's breasts were extremely humble. Where my firmness gave me shape, hers were mere nipples. I still preferred her endowments to my own. I preferred the natural softness of a woman to the firmness of a man. It wasn't fair. I did nothing particularly physical. In fact, I tried to be as languish as I could, in fear I would increase my masculine tone. Despite this effort on my part, my body was inevitably masculine. But I guess there's a dress for every figure.

We spent the evening trying on different dresses. I think we may have tried all of them on. Sissy was exhausted, she slouched on a tufted settee nipping on a cracker. "We should pick something out for you to take home."

I knew she was right. If I came home empty-handed, our father may see no point in letting me come back and I wanted to come back. I yearned to take home the black dress we first tried on together.

"I like the black silk dress Sissy."

"You didn't think I was too flat chested for it?"

"No, I think that's the one you should wear for our birthday party. The neckline is very flattering."

"What would I go as?"

"Um . . . I don't know a cat, a crow, a spider . . ."

She playfully swatted at me. "Yuck, really Ken, a spider."

I grinned. "I don't know, go as a dark-haired angel. That's what you'll look like."

"I like that. I could make wings. Okay, I'll get that one, but let's pick out something new for you to match me." She popped the rest of the cracker into her mouth and went over to the men's section.

She picked out a new waistcoat and pants for me which looked like the ones I had.

"You should pick something out for Athena," I suggested. "She has so few dresses . . . we should maybe get her at least a handful. Something that suits her congenial nature."

I had not told my sister the true extent of my relationship with Athena, but I'm sure she guessed at it. Twice or thrice, she had come into my room so early in the morning she nearly caught Athena still in my bed. I knew Sissy would approve. She was the one, after all, who had told Athena the stories about me—the stories that first made Athena fall in love with me. I only hesitated because I feared the more people who knew about Athena and me, the more likely it was that my father would come to know the truth.

I could trust Sissy with this secret, but I feared it would give Athena a false sense of security and she would let her guard down. If my father knew my intention was to marry Athena once I was twenty-one, he would send her away. Athena, though perfect in every way was not the kind of woman the heir to an empire married. In her stead, my father would marry me off to another heiress and expand the Dahl empire. I was only turning eighteen this year. Twenty-one was far away, I had to be careful. I could not bear Athena being torn from me.

"That's a good idea," Sissy said, returning to the racks of dresses. "I think her color is blue," she said, more to herself than me as she plucked out light colored dresses and placed them on the counter. Sissy was so quick selecting dresses for Athena it was as if she had had the same idea about getting something for her, but waited for me to suggest it.

When Sissy wasn't looking, I slipped a lip balm into my pocket from the cosmetic stand on the counter. I had been eyeing them from a distance, curious about them and desperate to try one in front of my star-trapped mirror.

She took another cracker. "You sure you don't want one? They're really good. They taste peppery."

"No, I'm fine."

"You should eat something. You're looking too thin. Father's noticed. I've overheard him telling Athena that several times now."

"I eat only when I'm hungry. I don't want to look like him."

She giggled, "Ken you will never look like him because you are you and you can only look like you."

"I want to look like *you*."

She took my hand and pulled me down next to her on the settee. "You do. If your hair gets any longer and you get any thinner, they will think there are two Dahl women. Well, besides Grandmama. I think at some point a woman grows so old they don't count anymore, like they become some other mystical being."

I smiled at the idea of being mistaken for Sissy. However, Madame Prospera's comment about me being a beautiful, young man reminded me how far off I was. No matter how beautiful I am, I could never be Sissy.

She hopped to her feet. "I guess we should ring the bell for Madame Prospera to tally up our bill, that is unless you can wait till tomorrow to give Athena her dresses."

I blushed, a heat blooming across my cheeks. Sissy was right. I couldn't wait. If Athena loved the bookmark, she was really going to love the dresses.

"I'm teasing Ken," she said, pulling the rope attached to the bell. "I like Athena. I like her with you, but I'm sure you already knew that."

"I hoped so."

"Be certain. You have my blessing. She's good for you. With her around I don't have to worry about you. It gives me more time to focus on my writing."

I inclined my face toward her in earnest. "Do you worry about me?"

"It's natural for siblings, more so for twins."

She pulled the bell again. It tinkled.

I hated the sound of bells. The sanitarium was full of them. The wake-up bell. The breakfast bell. The test bell. It went on and on. And then there were the bells that rang during testing. They would go off with such a rapidity they sounded like steaming teakettles.

* * *

I sat in a chair in the center of a white room waiting for Dr.

Tarri. He came in, my eyes lifted slowly to him. He pushed in a small, covered cart. My pulse galloped. I'd never seen this cart before. He always could tell when I was anxious, no matter how well I thought I masked it, he always knew.

"Nothing to be nervous about Kenneth," he said, pushing the cart to me. "Today we are testing your perception." He uncovered the cart to reveal a wooden chest. He opened it, the contents hidden from me by the lid. He pulled out a small bell, a jingle bell, the kind you see adorning a horse's holiday collar.

"What is this, Kenneth?"

"A bell."

He placed it on the side of the chest. He then pulled out a bell on a handle, the kind used to ring for servants. "What is this, Kenneth?"

"A bell."

He placed it outside of the chest next to the jingle bell. From the chest, he pulled out a tiny, squarish shape bell, the kind I've seen stitched to scarves for accents. "What is this, Kenneth?"

"A bell."

He placed the small bell outside of the chest and picked up the second bell, the one with the handle, and rang it. "You told me this was a bell, what if I told you, it was a chime? What would you say to that?"

I hesitated.

"Do not tell me what you think I want to hear but what you think," he said reassuringly as if there was no wrong answer.

"I would say, you are mistaken. It's a bell. A chime is the noise a bell makes."

His coal-colored eyes cast downward, darkening his face in shadows. He put the bell down.

"I answered wrong?" I asked, anxiously sitting up in the

chair.

Slowly his eyes lifted. They were dark and vacant. There was no soul there. "Perception is a powerful device. A bell and a chime are the same thing. A bell rings—a chime rings. A bell can chime. A chime can ring like a bell."

I shook my head impertinently. "It was a trick."

"No Ken, it was a lesson in perspective. It's logic. Just because you believe a bell and a chime are not the same thing doesn't make it true. You can try to justify it, but that does not change the empirical truth. Your justification was a sound attempt at trying to blur the lines of reality, but that still doesn't make your perception true. You perceive hearing voices that are not there. You cannot justify them. They simply don't exist. I will prove that point to you now."

He walked out of the room. A ringing commenced. Louder. Louder. Louder. The sound came quicker and quicker. I covered my ears, but the sound penetrated through my hands and head like a drill.

After what felt like an eternity, the ringing stopped. Dr. Tarri walked back into the room to find me on the floor in the fetal position. He pushed back my hair. "Don't cry Ken, it was for your own good."

* * *

Madame Prospera came through the door pulling me out of my reverie. I was glad, I didn't want to recall what happened next.

"Sorry to bother you."

"Not at all," she said, linking her arm with mine. "What can I help you with?"

"I would like to bring everything home tonight, if that's alright?"

"Of course. I'll take good care of you."

Dr. Tarri wiped a tear from my cheek. "Ken, you worked yourself into a stupor again over a little test. You know what happens when you cry." He tucked my hair behind my ears. "Maybe a private lesson in my office would be more helpful than a visit to the switchboard. Would you prefer that?"

I nodded, afraid if I spoke the tears would gush out. He wiped another tear. "Don't worry, I'll take good care of you."

* * *

Facing the inside cushion, I lay on my side on the couch in Dr. Tarri's office, while he got up to get his pipe.

The smell of smoke filled the room. "You did well with the lesson today, Ken."

I stared at the button in the center of the couch's faded brocade cushion. I had stared at the two holes in the center of that black button the entire time he was on the couch with me—stared into those two holes like they were the button's eyes and wondered what it perceived from its position. I wondered if it guessed at the truth—that, *beneath the pressure of torments such as these, the feeble remnant of the good within me succumbed.*

Dr. Tarri's compliment on a job well done confounded me. "If I did well with the lesson, then why am I being punished?"

"I didn't know having sex with me was a punishment."

I sat up, my hands moving to cover my nakedness. "It was offered to me as that. The switchboard or a private lesson in your office. But I suppose it's as you always say: '*Never to suffer would never to have been blessed.*'"

He exhaled. "You're clever Ken, too clever for your own good. In another life you would've made a good doctor." He took a puff of his pipe. "I did present it that way, but what we share is not a punishment." He sat down behind his desk. "You *did* do well with today's lesson. If you would've remained calm through the ringing, you would have passed. Your problem is you can't shut off your feelings. You have to learn to shut them off. For most people it's natural, for someone like you, it has to be learned. Your emotions fuel your psychosis. Oh Ken Dahl, if I teach you anything, I hope it's self-control."

CHAPTER SIXTEEN

Self-Reflection

In a near run I flung open the door to the cellar bathroom. I fumbled striking the match in my eagerness to get the candle lit. The candle was almost spent. I made a mental note to bring a new one down with me the following night.

As soon as the bathroom was bathed in the candle's glow, I opened my waistcoat and unbuttoned the remaining buttons of my shirt, folding the corners of the collar down to a plunging 'V'. I pulled the lip balm from my pants pocket. In my haste, I didn't look to see the color I plucked. My heart pounded with excitement, it was rose red.

I removed the lid of the tin. With the tip of my finger, I extracted some of the lip balm. Steadying my hand by locking my elbow against my chest, I applied the tinted wax. I rubbed it into my lips warming it with my fingers until it coated them. I puckered my lips like I had seen my grandmother do a hundred times, smoothing out the velvet color. My eyes slowly lifted to the mirror. The lip balm gave the illusion my lips were plumper than they were. They brought out my cheekbones. I looked thinner. My red lips evened the playing field. It made me look more like my sister. Sissy normally didn't wear lip balm. She didn't have to. It was a thing she reserved for special occasions.

I pushed my hair over my shoulders. "Better," I said with a smile.

I didn't feel guilty about stealing from Madame Prospera's. I was sure she was paid handsomely for the evening; instead, I regretted not taking any eyeshadow or rouge.

"You look beautiful, Ken," I said in my sister's voice, my imitation spot on.

"Thank you, Sissy."

I sighed. I wished I could walk out of the bathroom wearing bright red lip balm and ask my sister what she really thought. Playing dress up was one thing. Wearing makeup for the sake of wearing it was another. I'm sure she would understand, but my father wouldn't.

I washed the lip balm off, playtime was over. I was pleased my lips retained a rosy hue. I wondered if Athena would notice it tonight. They still felt waxy. I was positive, if she didn't notice the color, she'd notice the feel. Maybe she would like it and want me to wear it for her. I buttoned my shirt and waistcoat. It was late, Athena would be waiting for me in my room.

I smothered the candle flame with my fingertips.

It had become routine to look at myself in the small oval pin Athena gave me in the morning and visit the cellar mirror at night, returning to my room to find Athena waiting for me. We would talk and then we would climb into my bed, trying to understand each other by pressing our naked bodies together.

I understood Athena. In fact, I was sure of it. It was as I always thought. With understanding came love and the ultimate truth of my heart was and is that I love Athena. Although she was far from understanding me, she tried and that was more than anyone else had done.

By candlelight, I sat in my armchair waiting for Athena, eager for her to see the dresses Sissy had picked out for her. I glanced at my pocket watch; it was one in the morning. I was usually back in my room by midnight. I wondered what kept her. I would've gone to her room, but I wasn't sure which one was hers. I knew it was down the hall. I'd ascertained that much the first night I was home and she caught me coming back from the cellar. No, it was better to sit tight and wait.

I dozed off in my armchair. Hearing a soft knock on my door, I jumped to my feet. It was Athena. She rushed in whispering an apology. I hugged her, pressing her to my chest. "No matter," I said, reaching for the parcel from Madame Prospera's that rested by the side of my chair.

"For me?" she asked surprised, taking the package from me hesitantly. I nodded, not able to conceal the smile blooming across my face. She placed the large package on my bed and unwrapped it. Blue lace spilled out over her hands.

"Sissy picked them out. She has impeccable taste."

"Sissy . . ."

"Yes," I said, holding up the first dress for her to get a better look at it.

"Ken," she said in shock. "I've never seen such a beautiful dress."

I spread out the next dress for her. This one was lavender and cream with a high cream collar. Another in a mint, and a final gown of the purest white with white beads adorning the square neckline like a choker made of freshly fallen snow. The same beads followed the hem of its billowing skirts.

"This is my favorite," I said, running my hand over the white dress. "I want you to wear it for Sissy's and my birthday party. I think you'll look like an angel in it."

"I don't know what to say." She looked up at me with her blue eyes that appeared extra light in my dark room. The candle had burned out and the only light came from the sliver of the moon.

I grinned. "Usually when someone gives you a present, you say thank you."

She blushed, the color visible even in the dark. "Thank you. Thank you so much. I've never owned a dress close to one of these," she said, hugging them to her bosom. "These aren't even dresses, but gowns meant for a princess. I can't imagine wearing these in the kitchen."

"You won't have to," I said, taking her hand in mine. She looked at me puzzled, her eyes darting around my face but never landing on my pale-blue eye. "When I turn twenty-one, I inherit the estate. I will be master of this house."

"But your father—"

"My father is only custodian of Dahl House until I am of age. He is not a Dahl by blood and has no claim over the family fortune. The fortune goes to male descendants only. My great, great grandfather made it that way."

My confidence faltered in Athena's silence. I looked to the floor, saying more than I should. "He knows this, and I think it's part of the reason he sent me away. He can't do that now. His plan backfired, they sent me back and there's no way I'm leaving."

I shouldn't have diverted my eyes. I did nothing wrong. Dr. Tarri said, 'Innocent people do not look away'. That's right, I was innocent. I was sent away wrongly, I had nothing to be ashamed of. I was sane.

My eyes lifted to her face. "What I'm trying to say Athena is that you won't have to wear your dresses in the kitchen because you'll be the lady of this house. When I am of age, I want to marry you. I want you to be my wife." My words became hurried. "Of course, you can still look after the flowers in the solarium if that pleases you. But you won't have to work in the kitchen or wait on anyone, not even me. I don't want that for you. I want you to be my equal." Her lips quivered. "You already are, maybe more. I love you, Athena."

She threw her arms around me. I, in turn, did the same. I pressed her to me and kissed the top of her head. "For a moment there Athena, I thought you were going to reject me." I chuckled to myself. "No, I knew you wouldn't. I understand you." Kissing the top of her head again, I noticed the scent of smoke in her hair—not the stale smoke of the Burnt Wing but the pungent odor of imported cigars. The kind my father smoked.

I heard a voice; it started in a murmur, then grew louder. It was not the voice I associated with my mother, but a deeper one. A man's voice. "Ask her why she was late tonight, Ken."

I ran my hand down her curls before releasing her from my hug. I loved the feel of her golden wheat hair on my hands, it was softer than any silk. "Why were you so late tonight? What kept you?"

She folded the dresses on the bed, stacking them as neatly as she could as she spoke. "I had to tend to your father. He wasn't feeling well."

"Oh, I hope the old brute didn't give you too much trouble."

"No," she said, taking a seat on the bed.

"Good. I don't want to talk about my father." I sat down next to her, just missing the dresses. I pressed my lips to hers, wondering if she would notice mine felt different. I pulled away abruptly, it was *her* lips that felt different—foreign.

"Ask her why Ken," a different voice said.

"Athena, your lips . . . they feel different . . . why?"

"What?!" She said, wiping at them.

I ran my finger across her lips, they were swollen, rough even—severely chapped. "I hope you're not coming down with something."

"No, I'm just a little tired."

"Let me walk you to your room," I said, checking my pocket watch. I was surprised to see it was already well past three in the morning. "It's really late Athena, you should lie down." I ran my finger the length of her lips again. "I'm worried you're getting sick."

"I don't want to go," she said, her arms encircling my waist while she buried her head in my chest. Her words became muffled. "I want to be with you forever."

"I want the same," I said, meaning it. Athena had become part of me. I saw it when I looked at my face in the small mirror pin and the cellar looking glass. There was a sparkle in my eyes that was not there a few months ago. It was the confirmation of our love. The literal and physical expression of the inexpressible. I had never felt so full. I had the love of two women, and they both loved me back.

Another voice spoke to me. This one was shrill and whiny. "She doesn't love you, Ken. She's betrayed you. She slept with your father." My eyes darted around the room, knowing I wouldn't see anyone. I wrapped my arms around Athena, pinching myself. I hoped the pain it caused me would stop the voices, but it didn't.

"She told him she loved him."

I released my pinch, a bruise already forming on my hand.

"Athena, I have to ask you something."

"Yes," she said, her head still against my chest.

"I don't mean to come off crazy but . . . I'm hearing things and need to silence them." She lifted her chin, her blue stare falling on my face. "Athena, what exactly were you helping my father with tonight?"

Tears beaded on her thick lashes. "Like I said, he wasn't feeling well. I was just helping him get comfortable."

She was lying. I had learned all the signs of lying from Dr. Tarri. Learned all the cues that let him know when I had lied to him. Her glassy eyes, the way she held her fingers twisted into knots on her lap, and her hunched shoulders, were all tells.

I placed my hands on her shoulders and made her look me in the eyes. I made her look into my pale-blue eye that she was so keen on avoiding. "Tell me the truth Athena." I could feel her body tremble under my grip. I didn't care if I was hurting her, I held fast. "Tell me the truth, what were you doing with my father tonight? Why are your lips so chapped?"

"I . . . your father asked me to . . . I was . . . I was with your father."

"I need you to be more specific Athena. What were you doing with him?"

She burst into tears, crying into her hands. "I slept with him. Ken, I had to. I had no choice. I'm the only thing standing between you getting sent away again. He values my opinion. He loves me."

I sucked air. My heart throbbed as if it just cracked in half. The pain kept the voices at bay. Everything was silent, besides the beating of my broken heart and Athena's sobs.

Knowing it was his mustache that chapped her lips, made me want to tear her lips off her face. The thought of her lying naked in my father's arms as she whispered, 'I love you,' was more than I could stand. I got up, gripping my stomach. I dry heaved, but there was nothing to throw up. The room was spinning around me, I clung to my armchair to stop myself from falling prostrate. I felt Athena's hand on my arm. She was just like everyone else who claimed to love me—she used me.

"Ken, please try to understand."

I turned to her manic, my anger near insanity. "Try to understand?!" I said too loudly. She tried to shush me, to no avail. "I thought I *did* understand you! But no, how could I when you've lied to me this whole time. You said you loved me before you met me. I opened myself up to you and you've treated me like everyone else has. You betrayed me, Athena."

"No! I love you."

"No. No, you don't. You know how much I hate my father. If you loved me, you never would have—I can't bring myself to even say it."

I turned from her, biting my knuckles. I wanted to scream. I wanted someone to stop my heartache. I prayed for the pain of the electric shocks at Westminster. *Anything was more tolerable than this derision.*

Athena clung to my arm, weighing me down. I was near collapsing. "Ken, you don't understand, your father thinks you're still sick. I've been telling him you're well."

I faced her. "I *am* well," I said, in a voice that sounded a lot like my father's. "*I am well.* And I am seeing things clearly. You used me like everyone else. Like everyone else, but Sissy. It's always been for one thing or another. But you're no better than Dr. Tarri. You used me for sex, just like he did. That's what this was all about. Sex means nothing to me, I wanted a connection, I wanted love. I wanted to be understood."

I didn't care if she knew about Dr. Tarri or if she knew that I spent the last four years committed. None of that mattered now. I assumed as my father's confidant she knew it all anyway. The line about being sent abroad was just another one of her lies.

I plopped down in my armchair, covering my face with my hand. "All I wanted was love . . . but not you Athena. I can see that now. You're just a whore, sent to spy on me by my father. Shame on me for not understanding the real you . . . That's why he gives you books. They're payment for your services."

"No!" She said, dropping to her knees and throwing her arms around me.

I pushed her off. "I will not be used Athena. I promised myself, never again."

She sobbed at my feet. There was so much emotion. So many tears. How could so much feeling be false? Anyone looking in would've thought it was *me* who'd wronged her.

"Athena," I said in a whisper, now in control of myself. "I think you should return to your room. I've tried to understand you like I promised because you claimed to love me. But what you offer me are excuses for your behavior and I don't accept excuses."

"I do love you," she said in a gasping sob. "Let me prove it to you."

My anger surged again. Why wouldn't she just admit she'd lied to me? Lied when she claimed to love me. She had been keeping tabs on me for my father, her true sun. Why keep up the charade?

"You want to prove it?!" I said sharply, grabbing the spoon from the sugar bowl that sat on the small table next to my armchair. I seized Athena by the back of her head, pulling her off the ground. I shoved the spoon in her hand. "You want to prove it to me?!"

"Yes," she said, "I'll do anything."

"If you love me, you'll scoop out one of your eyes with that spoon. You'll be just like me then. You'll have one blue eye and the other will be a dark hole. Then maybe, just maybe, we will be able to truly understand each other."

She whimpered. "But . . . but I'll be ugly . . ."

"No," I said with a fierceness. "You will not be ugly. You will be more beautiful to me than ever. You will be my beautiful goddess. My own Pallas Athena. More infinite in your beauty than in your wisdom. Every time I look upon your face and see that dark hole where your eye used to be, I will know just how much you love me. Your missing eye will be an everlasting sign of your love for me. Your love and your faithfulness. And the whole world will see it. You will be bonded to me forever just like we both want. You are a violet Athena, and I am your sun. Yield to me."

She gripped the spoon with both of her hands, putting it up to her eye. "Ken, I can't."

I sneered, shaking my head. My love for her transformed to venomous disdain. "No . . . I didn't think you would—and it's Mr. Dahl to you now. But unlike my father, you're not welcome in my bed."

CHAPTER SEVENTEEN

The Plutonian Shore

I awoke to the sound of screaming. Still dressed in my clothes from yesterday, I rushed out into the hall. I never made it into my bed last night. I sat in my armchair gazing outside the window at the house's reflection in the lake until my eyelids finally closed and I submitted myself to sleep.

I saw Cook; she stood at the end of the hall dressed in her usual, a simple dress with a long apron double tied around her thick middle. Her screaming had ceased and was replaced with sobbing hiccups. I approached her slowly, not wanting to upset her more. Cook and I stood arm to arm. She pointed at the room in front of us, the door already ajar.

Sissy was by my side now, having also been awoken by Cook's screams. "What happened?"

I couldn't respond. My mind was taking longer for me to

understand what I saw than my eyes. I knew before I entered the room, she was dead.

On a bed of white sheets lay Athena. Under her head pooled a rutty red stain. The smell of blood was thick in the air. I entered her room, keeping my eyes on the stain. I knelt on the bed, gently turning her head. My heart skipped a beat. I wasn't breathing. I couldn't. Athena's right eye was missing. In its place was a dark pit clotted with congealed blood. The spoon I'd given her last night laid next to her on the sheets. "Oh no no no Athena," I said, looking into the void in her face. "Oh no Athena. My dear sweet goddess—no."

This was because of me. I did this to her. She'd scooped out her eye, digging the spoon in too deeply and accidentally killing herself. Sissy approached, touching my arm gently, just enough to let me know she was there. I became aware of other servants in the room, including Cook.

I unfolded Athena's little fist, expecting to see her missing eye but I only found a few strands of long, dark hair. I examined the hair closely. It looked like mine.

"What would have made her do such a thing?" Cook asked, wiping her tears with the inside of her apron.

I repressed a sad smile. "Love."

Athena had done it for me because she loved me. I asked her to prove her love and she did, and in turn, I killed her. *She had been made perfect in loveliness only to die.*

Last night I'd told Athena she'd be more beautiful to me with one eye removed for love than she was ever before. It was true. Athena never looked so holy. So otherworldly in beauty. Her skin was paler than any marble. Her yellow hair was almost golden in the sun filtering in through her bedroom window. It sat upon her head like a crown. Her lips were painted in blue as if frost kissed. Her remaining eye looked like a small planet, filled with the secrets of life. Never before had she held this much beauty. I was certain she was the real Pallas Athena.

And what a fitting place it was for her to die. On every surface of her bureaus were dried flowers. No doubt, these were the flowers taken from my meal trays and preserved here in her room awaiting her wake.

Athena loved me—really loved me. This realization shook my body. I wanted to scoop her up in my arms and kiss her bloody socket.

This was so much different than the way Dr. Tarri had killed himself. He too had claimed he loved me. He begged me to fail my final test and stay with him at the sanitarium.

My final test, like all patients at Westminster, was to be administered in front of a panel of clinic doctors, including the head of the sanitarium, Dr. Tarri. If I passed, I was sent home a sane man.

My final test was a simple one. Dr. Tarri and I both knew I would pass. He had taught me too well. They were going to show me a mirror and discern if I heard voices from it.

For a group of doctors who claim to be psychiatric experts, they didn't listen well. I never claimed to hear voices through mirrors. I had told my grandmother and father, I heard my mother's voice while gazing into a mirror. But adults, they never really listen to children. They took what they wanted from my words and twisted it, making mirrors a trigger for my psychosis.

I had spent the last four years making sure when the time came, I would pass my final test. Dr. Tarri had been studying me, but I was also studying him. All I had to do was remain calm. All of Dr. Tarri's tests had readied me for this, he had taught me to suppress my emotions, taught me how 'sane' people respond to stimuli, taught me to wear a mask. I couldn't fail. Not even Dr. Tarri could keep me at Westminster Sanitarium if the majority of the doctoral panel deemed me cured.

Knowing this, Dr. Tarri pleaded with me, in the name of love, for me to fail my final test. He begged me to fake a mental breakdown in front of the clinic's doctors. He described, in excruciating detail, all the things I should do to prove my insanity: from screaming, to tearing out my hair, to breaking the mirror with my fist.

I'd listened to him unmoved as he held my hand, tears streaming down his face in a way that could only have been described as insane. I'd told him, much like I told Athena, the cost. I was being cruel. I knew he no longer held power over me. It would take nothing short of a mental breakdown for me to stay at Westminster and I had always been sane.

Unlike Athena, I didn't care if Dr. Tarri loved me. I had not one ounce of love for him. Where Athena had been kind and giving, Dr. Tarri had only ever taken from me—taking my childhood, my pride, my innocence. At one time I was truly a daisy—but he plucked petal after petal until I was something very different.

"Dr. Tarri," I'd said to him. "I may be able to believe you love me if you proved it to me."

"Anything Kenneth."

"The galvanic battery you used to hook me to when I was first brought here, the one that's used to administer the shocks, do you remember it?"

He knew it well. It was one of his favorite toys. He'd shock me until I was too exhausted to move and then he'd force his healing caresses on me.

"I want you to hook yourself up to it and shock yourself. I want you to understand how it feels and if you can understand that, then maybe you can understand me. And maybe then, and only then, I can love you."

I had said it, never expecting him to do it. However, the next day Dr. Tarri was found dead in his office. I was among one of the patients and orderlies to find him. He had hooked himself up to the galvanic battery, clamping each of his nipples before administering the shock. Despite being set to the lowest amperage, his heart gave out and he died. He sat on his couch, his tongue swollen, lolling out the corner of his mouth like the beast he was in life.

Seeing him dead gave me great satisfaction. Knowing he shocked himself for me and that shock had killed him, gave me a sense of revenge. It was as if my finger administered the killing shock.

The clinic was in an uproar after Dr. Tarri's death. Some of his unprofessional relationships with his patients came to light. Whether the clinic knew about my relationship with Dr. Tarri, I was unsure, but they skipped my final test and signed my release papers.

Apparently in his own way, Dr. Tarri *had* loved me. But our relationship was not like the one I'd shared with Athena. I had willingly entered into love with her. With Dr. Tarri, I had no choice, it was forced on me. I had to do what he said, if I ever wanted to leave Westminster Sanitorium for Boys. No—Dr. Tarri never really loved me. Athena . . . Athena did, her corpse was living proof.

I kissed Athena's icy lips. "God bless you. Oh, God bless you."

CHAPTER EIGHTEEN

The Pale-Blue Eye

I stood in the cellar bathroom staring into the small mirror that hung over the sink. The mirror was the same. The same thin line traced its border, the same flowers were etched into its arched top. I looked the same in the mirror as I did the night before. It confounded me how everything was the same, but yet Athena was gone. The twinkle in my eyes, the very sparkle that let me know I was in love with her, was still there—unaware she was found dead in her bedroom this morning. It still shone like my eyes caught two stars keeping them trapped in orbit within my pupil—one star twinkling in a blue sky, the other in a night sky. Both eyes shielded by thick black lashes that sought to keep the love trapped in there forever. I wondered if my love for Athena would always burn there, or would it burn out? Even the brightest star eventually burns out. The sun too would one day cease to shine, and everything would be cold and dark and dead. Was it possible for my love for her to last forever? I couldn't lie to myself. My eyes told me the truth—forever was not long enough. When there was nothing left, I would still love Athena.

My goddess, my love, was not far. It was a short trip to the family vault from the cellar. I put my hand on the daisy wallpaper nearest to where she rested. I realized for the first time the wallpaper was embossed. As I thought, my hand traced the daisies, feeling every elevation of their petals, the curvature of their stems.

I had promised Sissy not to go to The Vault again, but she couldn't have known what would befall my sweet goddess. If she knew that, and knew the true depth of my feelings for Athena, she would never keep me from her. Besides, things are not always what they seem. As trivial as it was, the daisy wallpaper proved that to me. How much time had I spent in that cramped bathroom and I never touched it—never felt the texture under my palm until tonight.

My recent trip to the family vault could have been a similar experience. And then there was Dr. Tarri's lesson of the bells. 'Perception is a powerful device', he always said.

I had bumped my head rather hard that day, my perception of the subsequent events were feasibly askew. And then, there were the lost memories from my boyhood. Could I really trust them?

It was not rational for me to fear the family vault. Fear or rather unbridled fear, which was what I felt in relation to it, was one of the five cardinal vowels of insanity.

I hadn't had my chance to say goodbye to Athena and I wasn't going to let fear stand in my way. I was ushered out of her room by my father, and then the gardener along with the porter relocated Athena's body to The Vault.

I pulled out my matchbox and broke a match in half. Taking a deep breath, I pushed the broken match under my nailbed. The pain shot up my left index finger to my arm. I clenched my teeth to stop myself from groaning in pain. Blood welled under my nailbed spilling out in a steady drip. With a trembling hand, I wrapped my finger with the pocket square from my waistcoat.

There was no guarantee this pain would stop me from hearing voices. All day I had heard them on and off in an incessant murmur of white noise. They whispered amongst themselves and to me about Athena. I knew there was something about the family vault that gave the voices strength, perhaps even form. Maybe it was its proximity to Hell.

Sissy had her reasons when she made me promise not to return there. I felt compelled to take the necessary steps to protect myself, and thus employed Dr. Tarri's pain management for mania. If I couldn't hear the voices, I couldn't see the owners of them. If I was blind and deaf to whatever was in the family vault, whether it be good or evil, they couldn't hurt me and they couldn't stop me from seeing my Pallas Athena.

It all seemed very logical, and I felt assured my trip to the family vault would be without consequence. My finger—nay—my entire hand throbbed. It pounded as if it had its own little heart.

I took the candle from the crawl space window. I was going to need more than matches tonight. I bobbed and weaved over and under the wooden barricades making my way back into the main hall in record time. With the zeal of my boyhood, I bounded down the sloping passageways to The Vault. I again stood before the iron gates of Dahl Crypt.

The iron birds I once thought looked happy at being surrounded by plump berries seemed changed. Their steely eyes were dark and protruding, their sharp beaks menacing. It wasn't plump berries they were craving, but rather their beaks were made to tear flesh from bone like the beak of a vulture. "Unbridled fear is a sign of insanity. Unbridled fear is a sign of insanity. Unbridled fear is a sign of insanity," I mumbled under my breath.

Hesitating for only a moment, I unlocked the gate and let myself in. The gate pushed open with ease this time, barely letting out a sigh. Someone had oiled it.

I approached the top of the stairs with great care, waving the candle at the treads below me. Satisfied the stairs were clear of anything I could trip over, I descended. With my free hand, I clung to the damp wall for extra support. The lingering scent of stale smoke was pungent, stronger than I recalled it being a few short months ago. I took each step slowly and methodically, not wanting to risk slipping on a loose paver like before.

My every motion brought me closer to Athena, my heart sprinted as hers used to when she was near me. When I was safely down the stairs, I went to the marble platform. I was sure Athena would be there in the center of The Vault, high on the marble platform held up by cherubs to Heaven as my mother had been.

I was right. Inside the open marble coffin was Athena's casket. It was a beautiful casement of dark walnut inlayed with rosewood to form a lovely motif of flowers. The rich scent of the rosewood could be smelled over the damp and stale smoke of the fire long since put out.

I placed the candle on the edge of the platform and opened the coffin. The lid was heavy and well made. It took both hands to pry it open. I picked up the candle again, passing the flame over Athena. She looked like she was sleeping, much how she looked the first night I came into my room and found her on my bed. Her hair spiraled around her in a sea of gold. With her eyelids closed and her pale cheeks and lips the same shade of alabaster, she looked like a Greek statue.

Sissy insisted she'd be buried in the white gown she was to

wear for our masquerade birthday. As I hoped and feared, she looked like an angel in it. As if she just came from Heaven, the gown's crystalline beads gleamed in the light of the flame like stardust. Her skin was the same shade as the dress as if the fine satin was an extension of herself. The many layers of the material folded around her small body like spread wings. Her golden hair had always given her a divine halo, and in the eclipse of her casket shone.

Relinquishing the candle, I hugged Athena to my body. She was stiff with the rigors of death, her body no longer able to conform to mine. I sobbed into her soft hair. No one would know. Besides, even Dr. Tarri had cried at the thought of losing me and the love between us was one-sided. With Athena, we both *loved with a love that was more than love.* This gave me permission to cry—warranted it.

I was never really insane except upon occasions when my heart was touched. And I didn't care how insane I looked or even felt. I couldn't bear the idea of us being apart. But yet, we were already separated. I placed her body down gently, as if she was the most fragile thing in the world. I unwrapped the makeshift bandage around my finger, pulling the matchstick out from underneath my nailbed. Blood dripped onto Athena's dress marring its beauty with reality. I needed to hear her voice.

"Athena," I said to her, my hand holding hers. Her hand was like ice. It was so different now, though at first glance it was the same small hand it had always been. "Can you hear me? It's Kenneth."

The Vault was silent. Silent in a way few things can be. The whispering voices I had heard during my last visit to The Vault did not make themselves known. The family vault was indeed a cliché and was as silent as a tomb. Not the scampering of mice, nor the dripping of moisture down the outer walls, could be heard. Not even my own breathing gave way to sound. It was as if the entire vault stood apart from reality.

Yes, there was no whispering from the dead, though the gleaming nitre eyes, painted blood-red by the glow of my candle, still peered out from the shadows of the crypt like a jury of judges watching my every move. I was guilty. Oh, that I knew. I didn't need their judgment. I had already sentenced myself to a life of misery and regret. The guilt was mine as few things would ever be.

I grew hysterical at not hearing Athena's sweet voice. I tried to recall its perfect likeness and struggled. She was already so far from me, slipping further and further from my fingertips with every passing second.

Outbursts are a sign of insanity. Let it be known I am insane. "My beautiful goddess, I need you to know I'm sorry. Oh God, Athena why did you do it?! Why did you listen to me?! Love has made us both stupid and I am its greatest fool!"

I buried my head into her chest, her heart no longer beating for me. A cold hand brushed my hair back. I didn't move, I didn't want it all to be in my head. I wanted this touch to be real.

"Athena, is that you?"

A familiar voice answered me back. It was not Athena's but the voice I knew as my mother's. "I am sorry Kenneth."

Reluctantly, I pulled myself from Athena's bosom. Hovering next to Athena's coffin, in the same glowing white gown, was the faceless woman. But her shadow face was more than a shadow. A bloody pale-blue eye hung from it.

"Jesus!" I shouted, pushing myself back and away and landing on the floor.

I heard my sister's voice in my ear as if she was right next to me. "Kenneth run! And don't come back down here!"

I left the candle, not wasting the time to go back for it and darted up the stairs. I closed the gate to the family vault, struggling to lock it.

Finally getting the key to twist, and hearing it lock, I looked up to see the woman again. Her face, along with the bloody eye, was pressed against the bars of the gate as if she couldn't pass it. I knew that eye. It was Athena's. I stumbled back almost tripping over my feet.

The woman reached her small hands through the bars of the gate. "Kenneth, don't leave. I love you."

The blood from Athena's eye dripped onto her glowing gown as if it had just been torn from Athena's socket. The smell of fresh blood overtook me, wobbling my legs. I leaned against the corridor wall for support.

"You're not here. You're in my head, and I know how to make you go away," I said shakily, keeping my eyes on her and feeling for the matchbox in my pants pocket. "Illusions are a cardinal vowel of insanity and I'm *not* insane."

I took a match and pressed it under my nailbed. Once secured, I jammed my left middle finger into the stone wall. The match cracked under my nail, blood springing from my finger. I winced in pain, holding my lame hand with my good one—the woman was gone.

CHAPTER NINETEEN

Dust from the Earth

The rain fell in a soft pitter-patter on my umbrella. I felt as if I was hearing nature's own tune reserved for the world human beings can't see or hear—the music of the leaf flute, the mushroom bongo, the rain harp. It was as melancholy as it was lovely. I wondered if Athena, wherever she was, could hear it—could hear me—hear my thoughts and know I missed her.

It was time to lower Athena's casket into the ground. My body tensed, sending the little hairs on my arms and neck standing on end. I didn't want her to be inhumed. I would've most likely stopped the whole thing if Sissy wasn't clinging to my arm sharing my umbrella. Sensing my agitation at what was to come, Sissy squeezed my arm, her soft cries mingling with the raindrops in their dirges.

Sissy was right of course. I had to stand steadfast. This was the way of the living—our beloved dead, we bury. With eyes as glassy as the water beaded on her casket, I watched Athena's body disappear into the earth below, the words of the priest ringing in my ears.

"And God formed dust from the earth into a man and he blew into his face a breath of life, and the man became a living soul. . . . To dust you shall return . . . We therefore commit this body to the ground, earth to earth, ashes to ashes, dust to dust; in sure and certain hope of the Resurrection to eternal life."

As the casket lowered, the cries rose. Cook was hysterical and my father, he too, wept aloud. I had never seen him cry like that. It appeared he *did* love Athena. She'd been right about that. Everyone at Dahl House loved Athena. There was not one dry face, besides my own. But I'd shed my tears last night, crying myself to sleep against my closed bedroom door. Even now, in the face of burying my beloved goddess, I had to wear a mask.

Athena's fatal flaw was that she loved me. She loved me and I tested her. Tested her like Dr. Tarri had tested me time and time again. Athena had promised to never test me, if only I would have made her the same promise. You don't test people you love. You just love them. I wished I had learned that lesson before I pushed that damnable spoon into her hand and asked her to prove her love. Love had killed my beautiful Pallas Athena, and I was to blame.

Guilt weighed me down. The rain hitting the umbrella might as well have been boulders. I killed my beautiful goddess. Just as I had killed my grandmother's cat Pluto. And one could argue, as I killed Dr. Tarri. I killed them in the name of love. To love me meant death. I knew that now.

My family, along with the servants, went inside. I stayed and watched the gardener shovel the dirt on top of Athena's casket. With each crushing sound of dirt hitting the wood coffin, she moved further from me. She may be returning to dust, but I was still there. *And then there stole into my fancy, like a rich musical note, the thought of what sweet rest there must be in the grave.* I wished I could crawl inside her coffin and be put to rest with her—becoming dust and bones with her.

But we would never rest with each other. Athena was being buried in the east-end of the cemetery. The east-end was reserved for non-family members. Athena would rest amongst the servants who died during the fire of 1821 and other servants who had served the House of Dahl.

When I die, I will be buried at the west-end of the cemetery with my mother. It seemed a poetic justice to be so close to Athena, but yet, so far away. As it was for us in life, it would be in death.

I continued to wait graveside as the earth covered Athena one shovel at a time. When the gardener was done, he smoothed out the freshly spread dirt with his spade. I placed the red rose I had been holding, its thorns piercing through my gloves in blissful pain, on the ground. It was a symbol of my sin and my love. It was the best rose the solarium had to offer and I placed it over her feet like a faithful supplicant.

I made my way to the arched gates of Dahl Cemetery. The ironwork reminded me of the gates to the family vault, it too was plentiful with sharp beaked birds, plump berries, and jagged leaves. The uneasiness from last night crept back in. A chill ran up my spine, forcing me to close my greatcoat. I sped through the archway not making eye contact with one iron-formed bird, the umbrella giving me a false sense of protection as I scurried through.

Once through the archway, I turned around to get one last look at Athena's burial site and noticed my grandmother standing at the west-end of the burial grounds.

"She must be visiting her brother's grave," I muttered to

myself.

I couldn't imagine losing my twin like she had—to be separated from the one person who was born to understand you. I had lost Athena, but I still had my beloved twin sister. She had always been my foundation, my strength. I could weather any storm, including the storm that came and took my Pallas Athena from me, as long as I had Sissy.

My grandmother, perhaps feeling my eyes on her, turned to see me. I waited on the other side of the archway for her. Together we looked back at Dahl Cemetery, my eyes on the east-end, hers on the west-end.

"They're ravens, you know?" she said, glancing up at the beady-eyed birds above our heads.

"Ravens?"

"Yes. The raven signifies transformation."

"To dust . . ."

"I hope to something more Kenneth," she said, taking my hand and squeezing it.

We made it back to the house just as Cook set out the hors d'oeuvres. From the disgruntled mutterings of hungry servants, I was able to put together that Cook had forgotten to turn on the oven before attending Athena's funeral. Everyone returned to the house to uncooked food. But now that piping hot platters were being placed on the main dining hall table, the servants seemed not to have minded the delay. They whispered merrily between themselves, wondering if Cook had intentionally forgotten to turn on the oven as a means to get more time off.

Under normal circumstances the servants would not have gathered in the main hall after a servant funeral service, but in their own dining hall made of old stone. Because Athena had endured herself to her masters, the exception was made.

The servants congregated in the large room seemed fewer in number than they'd appeared graveside. There, they loomed over the headstones like specters themselves. Here, amongst the faded tapestries and chairs, they looked just as worn and old. The only one of them who had youth and beauty was Athena, and in her absence they all looked dead, stuffing their corpses with pastries and meat pie.

Besides the priest, there was another man there who I recognized from my past. He was older now, with a thick, auburn beard, but I knew him to be a doctor. When I'd laid comatose in my bed after taking the spill down the steps of the family vault, he was there every day, applying healing balms and rubbing my lips with lifesaving elixirs.

I shrank from him. Just knowing he was a doctor made me feel uncomfortable as if he held the key to locking me away again. I stood against the *Hunt of the Unicorn* tapestry—the unicorn trapped in a huntsmen's cage and me trapped in the room. My eyes darted from face to face searching for Sissy.

"Hey," she said, locking her arm in mine. "You need to eat something."

"I'm not hungry."

"All the same, you need to eat something."

I liked the dull ache I felt in my stomach. It worked two-fold. It helped keep the voices at bay and it also gave me something to control. While everything else spun out of control around me, things I could not change or affect, I still was in control of what I put into my stomach.

"Ken, just one bite."

I wasn't in the mood to be lectured and Sissy was nothing if not persistent. She knew I hadn't eaten since yesterday. With Athena no longer with us, no one brought us breakfast. I reached for one of those pastries the servants were making a big deal about. Cook couldn't keep them on the plate. I popped it in my mouth. Sissy kept her eyes on me while I chewed as if I was going to turn around and spit it out when she wasn't looking. It was filled with sweet cheese and was quite good. I wasn't going to tell Sissy that, she would want me to eat another one.

"It's a shame to see a beautiful girl like that die so young," the doctor said to Cook who worked on replenishing the plate of sweet cheese pastries. One by one, she took a pastry off her plate and placed it onto the platter on the table. It would have been easier for her to switch out the plates, but I reasoned she did that because the plate on the table matched the rest of the dishware being used.

"What do you think made her do it?" Cook asked.

I turned toward Sissy, my direct back facing the doctor and Cook. I didn't want to hear how I snuffed out Athena's light.

The doctor, with a mouthful of what I assumed to be fresh pastry, said, "I'm not sure what would make a sweet creature like that gouge out her eye, but something scared her to death."

I turned around, losing all anonymity. "What are you talking about? I thought she died as a result of the injury to her eye."

"Mr. Kenneth Dahl," the doctor said, extending his hand to me as if he had been waiting this whole time for my recognition. Apparently, he also recognized me, despite my growth spurt and my pubescent, beveled chin. "Good to see you well."

I shook his hand quickly—too quickly, forgetting all the hard learned lessons from Westminster Sanitarium. "Tell me what you know about Athena's death."

"Well, the trauma to the face was obvious, but superficial. What done the little lass in was her heart. It stopped."

"Can you be sure? Did you perform an autopsy?"

My father's eyes shifted to me. Post-mortem discussion

clearly made him uncomfortable. I had told him, when he found me with Pluto and the other cats, that I was performing an autopsy.

I burned with desire. I wish I had known Athena's heart had stopped. I would've performed my own postmortem examination using Cook's knives if I had to.

If what the doctor said was true, and Athena died because her heart stopped, I would be absolved of guilt. Her death would not be because of me, and her love would be no less certain. Oh heavenly Father, to know she had taken her eye out for me, to prove she loved me, and died from another cause unrelated to my unnecessary test, well, that would resurrect my spirit.

"Wasn't necessary," the doctor said, popping another pastry into his mouth.

My heart sank. Without an autopsy, I could never be certain.

"How did you know then?" Cook asked, leaning in as if to hear a bit of gossip.

"I saw it in her eye."

Cook whispered as not to upset anyone. "The one she pulled out?"

"No not that one. Funny enough that one was never found."

Cook's mouth dropped, her chins smacking against her chest.

"Not to worry, things like that always turn up sooner or later. Just last week, I found a finger I had misplaced a month ago." He chuckled, "I shut it in my notebook and forgot all about it. You see it was this teeny, tiny pinky finger." He cleared his throat realizing that no one found the matter funny. "Excuse me, we doctors have a lonely profession. Most patients are dying or dead. But as I was saying, I saw it in her eye, but uh, the other one. Her pupil was completely dilated. You see that because of two reasons. Fear or—"

"Love," I said, completing his sentence.

He smiled at me. "That's right, Mr. Dahl. Fear or love. It's funny those two emotions elicit the same response in the human eye."

"Yes, I always thought so too."

I wanted to inform this charlatan of a doctor that a postmortem of a heart that suddenly stopped would've revealed an enlarged heart, dilation of the heart's chambers, and the breakdown of vessels supplying blood to the heart. These findings, alone, could rule out love as the cause of death, leaving only fear. I could have smothered him with pastry balls until he choked, but given my history of presumed mental illness, I controlled myself.

The doctor went on, enjoying the attention of the small crowd that now surrounded him. "To be honest, I only ever saw this happen once or twice in a patient so young. It could've been hereditary. She could've had a weak heart. Women tend to be weaker of heart than men and it's easy to scare them to death. Especially a woman with a delicate constitution like Athena Lee."

The priest, who had remained silent as the doctor spoke, nodded his head in full agreement. I heard enough. This so-called doctor was not a man of science. He'd fit in well at Westminster.

Cook wiped tears on the inside of her apron. "May the angels above usher her to heaven."

"No," I said too loudly, gaining my father's attention again. "I want her to stay here in the house."

Sissy squeezed my arm. "Easy now, father's watching."

The doctor smiled, not unkindly. "Well, I'm sure with a girl like that, a little piece of her stays with all of us."

"I will drink to that," Cook said, taking a swig from a canteen she had tucked in her apron's pocket.

CHAPTER TWENTY

Every Rose Has a Thorn

Sissy went to the library to write. I, not being allowed in the library on account of my father thinking books would give me the irrational ideas of my youth, slipped into the solarium. I was never fond of the solarium despite my love of flowers. I didn't like how the humid air weighed down my hair making it stick to my forehead. There was something about the way the moist air suspended even the slightest breeze, making it hard to breathe in. It was as if it trapped the very essence of every living thing in there, filling the space between air and matter with the pungent aroma of earth. Every inhale intoxicates you, leaving you quite senseless by the time you leave.

I much preferred the fresh air of the outdoors. One could be at peace among the berries of the boxwoods in winter, the daffodils sprouting by the lake in spring, the blooms of the wisteria vines in summer. And of course, not that they were outside but located in the innermost part of the house, where everything was more real than the outside world, was the solace of the daisies in the cellar bathroom.

But the solarium was Athena's favorite room in the house. She had spent all of her free time there. She had taken over management of it when she was first brought on as a servant, relieving a more than willing gardener of the job. When I was not with Sissy, I would sneak into the solarium to surprise Athena. She liked those moments best when we could be together without the shadow of night—be together in what she called Heaven's moon—the sun. That's what I was to her—Heaven's moon: Helios, the living embodiment of the sun, giver of all life. Oh, how I have fallen from grace. Now I was the giver of death.

When I was still the sun, her eyes would sparkle, and she'd take my hand and show me what she was working on. She'd point out all the little things she was learning in her horticulture books, letting me read them despite my father's book ban.

I did like seeing Athena during the day in the solarium amongst the thriving trees and plants. We were like the biblical Adam and Eve. I would miss those moments more than anything. It was the closest to what life would have been like if we didn't have to hide.

I had decided that morning while I cut a rose for Athena, I would do that for her every day as she had cut a flower for me every morning to accompany my breakfast. It was my turn to return the favor and I was happy to do so.

I knew from watching Athena, there was more to maintaining the solarium than just clipping flowers and I was eager to learn all I had to. I picked up Athena's pocket size book on roses. I had seen her use it before to make a cut. I opened her book to see the embroidered bookmark I had given her. I ran my fingers over the violets. The thread felt as smooth as her hair. Having something she touched at my fingertips consoled me better than all of my tears the night before. The crackpot doctor was right, it was like a little piece of her was still there with me. She loved that bookmark, and I loved her.

As if guiding me, the bookmark marked the page I needed.

"Ah, I see, the correct way to prune a rosebush is on a diagonal between thorns." I picked up the pruning shears.

"There you are," my father said.

I was so engrossed in Athena's book, I didn't hear him enter the solarium. The solarium was constructed of large glass panels that interlocked with each other through metal casements. It was as wide as it was tall, standing two stories high. Despite not hearing my father enter, it was easier to hear through the glass panels as the only sound proofing was the greenery, than it was to see into it. The solarium was thick with exotic plants, fruit trees, and rare flowers. Walking into it was like entering a tropical oasis.

"Here I am."

"What on Earth are you doing in here?" he asked, wiping his clammy forehead with the back of his arm. "I hate the solarium."

I resolved at that moment to love the solarium as Athena did. More so now, by virtue of my father hating it.

"I'm pruning a rosebush."

Ignoring me, he swatted at a white orchid that hung down from a planter near him. "I gave the servants the rest of the day off."

"That was kind of you," I said, relocating the orchid before going back to the rosebush.

He exhaled loudly as if he was expecting me to say something specific and didn't get what he wanted. "Ken, you're going to have to level with me."

My fingers tensed around Athena's book. "Level with you . . . I don't quite follow."

"Are you okay?"

My eyebrows lifted. "Me, yes—why? Are *you* okay? You seemed rather upset at the funeral."

Raking me over with his cold slate eyes, he ripped Athena's book from my hands. "What's this? I thought I said no books."

"It was Athena's. It's just a harmless book on pruning."

He examined it to make sure I was telling the truth. He ran his thumbs over the green linen cover. "Athena will be hard to replace. She knew just how I took my coffee."

"Yes," I said, faking a smile on his behalf. "She was very observant . . . and trustworthy," I added. I had to believe Athena when she said she was the only thing standing between me being sent away again. She had told the truth about my father loving her and had told the truth about loving me. I would take everything Athena said as the empirical truth. My father, following me into the solarium and questioning my wellbeing, proved he wanted me gone.

"Yes, she was," he said, looking at me expecting to see a crack in my mask.

"What happened to your hand?" He relinquished the book on the potting table, taking my left hand. He turned it over in his clammy palms. My two fingers were bruised to the first knuckle from the force of the matchstick being jammed under my nailbeds.

"Yesterday morning, I shut my hand in the door. Cook's screaming woke me from a deep sleep. I was half dazed, trying to get out to the hall as quickly as possible and accidently shut the door on my hand."

Again, my father interrogated me with his eyes, his gray pupils scanning over me like a laser. My lie was perfect—maybe too perfect—maybe too rehearsed. I could tell, despite the plausibleness of my story, he didn't believe me.

"I heard you were the one who found Athena."

My hand now free of his, I trimmed a branch of the rosebush, cutting between two sharp thorns. "Cook found her. I think we all must have heard her screams, even you Father. I was just the first to get there."

"That must have been a lot to see for a man with your condition."

I inclined my head toward my father. "My condition?" I was not shying away from this. I had nothing to hide. I was as sane as the next man. "*You fancy me mad?*"

He dodged the conversation, like the coward I always knew him to be. Before he sent me to Westminster, he couldn't say it to my face, couldn't tell me as he looked me in the eyes, that he thought I was mad.

"I'd understand if you weren't feeling up to having your birthday party."

"You're canceling it?" I asked, knowing how upset Sissy would be.

"I didn't say that. I just want to make sure you're feeling up to it."

"I feel fine. I'm sorry for what happened to Athena, but as far as I'm concerned, I'm fine."

My father traced the buttons on his waistcoat as his finger made its way down his barreled belly. "Okay, because if you need help Ken, I want to get it for you. I know we haven't always seen eye to eye, but we're all we have left."

I let him think that—that it was the two Dahl men against the world. As soon as I was of age, I would rip the estate from my father and ensure Sissy got the inheritance she deserved. No woman, especially a Dahl, deserved to be under the thumb of a man, and especially not my father's.

"Yes, father we are the last of the Dahl men and I want to be on the same page as you. So please have a little trust in me when I say I'm fine."

His index finger traced the button dab in the center of his waistcoat, his finger going around and around the opalescent pearl. "It recently reached me that the doctor, the head doctor at Westminster, committed suicide right before you came home. Uh, what was his name . . . um, Dr. Tarri."

"I am aware of Dr. Tarri's passing, but I thought his death was accidental."

"Well, that's just the rumor. But I suppose if you hang around the insane enough, you become insane yourself."

I pursed my lips.

"I have to ask . . ." my father said, lowering his eyelids to the potting table that stood between us. "Did you have anything to do with his death?"

With furrowed eyebrows I said, "Me, with Dr. Tarri's death? Of course not. Father, uh, I don't think you understand how a psychiatric hospital is run. It's like a prison but in place of bars there's padded rooms. Every time I left my room, I was escorted by a team of two. Two orderlies, a doctor and an orderly, or on the rare occasion two doctors. I was escorted back to my room in the same fashion. I mean father, what are you asking?"

He rubbed the top of his head in thought, his already disheveled gray hair, standing on end. "It's just . . . first the doctor and now Athena."

"Father, Athena's death wasn't a suicide."

"She removed her eye, the doctor was certain of that, no one did that for her. Why would she do that if she wasn't trying to kill herself?" he asked.

"I'm going to answer your question with a question. Why would Athena or Dr. Tarri, for that matter, commit suicide because of me?"

My father and I locked eyes. He truly looked at me for the first time since I came home.

"You're different Ken."

I smiled. "Of course, I'm different. The last time you spoke to me I was a thirteen-year-old boy. I'm not sure what you expected to see when I came home."

"You're right of course. A lot of time has passed. You were always such a sweet boy, maybe a little confused at times, but a sweet little boy. And now . . ."

"And now?" I repeated, honestly curious at what he thought of me.

"And now you're just . . . well you're just . . . I don't know, you're just not right."

I didn't like the turn this conversation was taking. My father was as pigheaded as they came. I knew I would not be able to change his mind about me with a few words. It was best to appease him, so he would leave feeling validated.

"It's going to take time for us to get to know each other again, but for now, we can both agree I'm not scary."

"No, that's not what it is. You're not scary."

"And the doctor said Athena's heart stopped. He said it in front of the entire household, he thinks she was scared to death. Could you really see me scaring someone? Let alone to death?"

My father shook his head. "No . . . no, you have that beauty about you that you share with Sissy and your mother. The three of you always reminded me of dark-haired angels."

It unnerved me to hear him refer to us as dark-haired angels. It was something I often said to Sissy, and she would say back to me.

It had no place coming from his lips.

He twisted the end of his mustache, twisting it to a point. "You didn't get that from me. No, scare someone to death, not you . . ." His eyes diverted to Athena's pruning book. "Sorry Ken, I guess Athena's death has affected me more than I care to admit. Suicide made more sense to me than being scared to death. What could have done that? . . . A rat maybe?"

I took the opportunity, for that was what it was, to steer the conversation toward the faceless woman. I normally would never have approached the subject with my father. Illusion was one of the five cardinal vowels of insanity, and what's more insane than claiming to see a ghost? But I, a person sane in mind and spirit, had spent last night sitting against my closed door, half too exhausted to climb into bed, the other half of me thinking it was safer to stay there in front of my door as a barricade.

"The barber did mention to me that the townsfolk think the house is haunted."

My father did not burst into laughter at hearing the rumor as I had, instead his demeanor hardened. This change baffled me. He stood uncomfortably upright, as if he were a soldier awaiting a uniform inspection. He stood before me several inches taller, though I was still his superior in height.

"That's preposterous. Our house haunted, I've never heard something so ridiculous."

"Yes, that's what I said. But still, he *was* afraid to be in the house. He has even mentioned, on more than one occasion, mind you, that when the weather turns nice again, he'd like to shave me outside."

"Superstitious lot, barbers are. I've never seen the woman in white."

I had not mentioned a woman in white. In fact, I had not

mentioned the house being haunted by a woman. I assumed the faceless woman and the woman in white were one in the same. She was, after all, in a glowing white gown, but as fantastical as that was, it was her absence of a face that drew my attention.

As if reading my mind he asked, "Have you visited The Vault, Ken?"

"Hmm . . . what? No, why?" I asked, pruning another branch of the rosebush.

"The gardener said a candle was left down there."

"Not mine, that's no place for me."

"Good. Stay out of The Vault."

It was evident the faceless woman had been seen by more than me. She was real and not a chimera, a figment of my supposed psychosis. And that meant her voice was real too. Confirmation—I was and am sane.

It had to be the faceless woman who scared Athena to death. She had Athena's eye, it hung from her shadow face as a trophy. Whether Athena's death was an accident or intentional, I would most likely never know the truth. But Athena being scared to death by a ghost didn't explain the dark hair I found in her balled fist—and didn't explain the lock on the family vault. Ghosts are intangible, they can move between matter, or can't they?

"Father, why is there a lock on The Vault?"

In a flash, his cheeks reddened, dark blotches spreading over his face and neck. "I thought you haven't been down there!?"

"I haven't."

He snatched Athena's book. "Don't go in The Vault. And no books. And tomorrow you're getting a haircut. I'm sick of seeing your hair like that. You're not a girl Ken. Start acting like a Dahl."

"I *am* a Dahl," I said, standing my ground. "It's you who's the outsider. When I come of age, you will feel that all too keenly."

My father pushed his belly over the potting table, our noses almost touching as he stood on his tippy toes. "Are you threatening me Kenneth?!"

I bit my tongue, blood pooled in my mouth. The pain helped me to regain control, stopping me from saying something I would later regret.

"I will have you thrown back in the sanitarium before the week's end if I think you're threatening me! One word about what happened here, and the doctors would be licking their chops to have Kenneth Dahl back and see their pockets lined in silver again. We both know if the doctors declare you incompetent, I remain in control of the estate. I will have you locked away until the day you die boy!"

Tears stood in my eyes. I called on all of Dr. Tarri's lessons to stop them from spilling over. I didn't doubt my father would send me back to the sanitarium. He had been fishing for a reason the whole time we were talking.

"No Sir, I'm not threatening you."

My father backed off. Once again, I could breathe.

"Good, like I said, we're the last."

He turned to leave.

I swallowed the blood sitting in the back of my throat, the iron taste, its own healing balm. "Wait Father . . ."

He reluctantly turned around. "What is it now?"

"Please don't make me cut my hair."

He exhaled like a wild boar ready to charge. "Damnit, why not Ken?"

I didn't have an answer he would understand. I told him the basic truth of it as I had told Dr. Tarri. "Because it reminds me of Sissy."

"Fine, keep your hair, but I keep this," he said, waving

Athena's book at me.

"I nodded graciously. "Thank you, Father."

"Tie it back at least, make it look presentable."

"Yes Sir," I said, twisting my long hair behind my back.

"And with Cook off the rest of the day, dinner is whatever is left in the dining hall. Make sure you eat something."

"Yes, of course."

"Because I'm telling you now, if you lose any more weight, you'll be going straight back to Westminster."

CHAPTER TWENTY-ONE

The Mighty Wings of a Raven

I placed a black orchid on Athena's grave and retrieved the bouquet of primroses I had placed there the day before. The primrose symbolizes the inability to live without your loved one. But somehow, I went on living. If only barely living. I followed Athena's example, saving all of the flowers I had given her in my room. The primroses would rest on Athena's pillow.

A small wooden cross had been placed as her grave marker while we awaited the arrival of her permanent headstone. Cook had carved her name into it with a knife from the kitchen. Its construction was crude and primitive, but heartfelt. Bright ribbons in red, purple, pink, and yellow hung from the arms of the cross as if she had died a child. I suppose that was true. *She was a child, and I was a child.*

There was something about the way the colored ribbons

blew in the monotone graveyard that made her death seem all the more tragic. She was the beauty and color in Dahl House and now she would be that for Dahl Cemetery.

The black orchid, the rarest of the flowers in the solarium, seemed a proper token of my love for today. It was the embodiment of the rare and coveted love we shared, the passion few get to feel in their lifetime. Today marked the one-week anniversary of her death. It bothered me how time moved on while I was still in the past. Tomorrow was my eighteenth birthday, there was no stopping it. Just as crab grass had sprung up around her cross, and in preparation for her headstone and ground plaque, gray cobblestones had been placed over the ground she rested beneath, things inevitably changed. I was careful not to step on these stones. I didn't like the idea of walking over my love. She did not belong under my feet but by my side.

The tree behind her cross rose up high above me. Its trunk forked directly in the middle slitting the tree in half. Its two branches fell to the side casting a shadow around us like the mighty wings of a raven. I had noticed this solitary Poplar tree from my sitting room window but did not take notice of it at her funeral. Perhaps, because the priest had stood in front of it or perhaps it was the rain. But I couldn't help noticing it today and thinking of what my grandmother said about the raven symbolizing transformation.

I pulled off my glove and unbandaged my middle finger, releasing the pressure of the matchstick that rested under my nailbed. I was just about to call out to Athena when I heard a voice I didn't recognize behind me.

"Do you believe in Heaven Sir?"

Thinking it was one of the voices only I could hear, I didn't bother to turn around or answer it. Dr. Tarri had told me answering the voices back gave them power over me. Without power, they would stop. It was one of his more logical approaches to dealing with my 'psychosis'. But it didn't work like the pain did.

I knew the voices were not the result of mental illness. My father seeing the faceless woman, without a shadow of a doubt, proved that, but Dr. Tarri's tactics, as much as I hated to admit it, worked.

The voice went on. "I think if there is a Heaven, Athena was the closest thing men like us can get to it."

I turned on my heels to see the coachman. It was the first words he had ever spoken to me. "I believe in Hell," I said. "I've been there . . . but I imagine you're right, Athena *was* the closest I will ever get to knowing Heaven."

He nodded, holding onto his hat as he dipped his head. "Your mother always said it was the curse of the Dahls to only know Hell. She said it was because of the eye."

"Eye?"

"The eye." He lifted his finger to my face. "Your mother had the same pale-blue eye your sister and you were born with. She said it was evil. That it let her tap into things she shouldn't be able to tap into. That it let her do things she shouldn't be able to do."

I evaluated him with the eye he claimed my mother said was evil. He turned from me, not wanting to meet its blue gaze. I suppose he got enough of it the day he brought me home.

"I didn't think anyone who still worked at Dahl House knew my mother. I thought everyone perished in the fire."

"All did perish in that fire Sir. All but me."

"And you knew my mother well?"

"Very well. I had just started as coachman to Dahl House when your parents got married. She handpicked me for the task, refusing to allow a footman to accompany us. She wanted only me. I drove her everywhere, including to the sanitarium right after you and your sister were born."

"Sanitarium? What are you talking about? My mother died bringing Sissy and me into the world."

"That's just what he told you."

I recalled the voice at dinner the first night I arrived home. 'You're not the first Dahl to enter the sanitarium.'

"So it's true then, I'm not the first Dahl to have been institutionalized."

He kept his body on a diagonal from mine as he spoke. "Before it was called Westminster for Boys it was Westminster for Families."

"For families?"

"It was a coed hospital for patients of all ages. Westminster ran into legal problems when they couldn't hide the high number of pregnancies amongst the patients. They fired most of the staff and changed into an all-boy facility to avoid any more scandals."

I squeezed the bouquet of primroses. "They should have closed it completely."

"I think they would have," the coachman said, "but it was backed by Dahl money. Instead of closing, the clinic reinvented itself."

"Dahl money? We pay for that prison?"

He nodded, gripping his hat brim again. The half of his face visible to me was cast in shadows thanks to his hat, but that didn't stop me from studying his face. The deep grooves by his mouth, told me he was old, weathered like his skin. The eye I could make out was dark and luscious, and filled with emotion that he kept trapped in his soul.

"Your father had legal control of the estate when your mother was admitted. By then, your grandmother's twin brother was confined to bed. He'd given your father power of attorney until he was well, or you were of age.”

I had underestimated my father. My mother was committed and so was I, before I could take control of the estate. My father probably meant to keep me at Westminster my entire life but the reinvention of the institution for the most part worked. The only doctor I had known to abuse their power was Dr. Tarri. But my father could send me back to the asylum without a concrete reason. He owned the place, and I was sure there was more than one corrupt doctor at Westminster. It was in his benefit to have me placed back in a padded room before I turned twenty-one.

“Your mother, she asked me on the way to Westminster, to put out her eye. She thought it would solve all of her problems, cure her inflictions.”

It saddened me to learn my mother and I were not alike. I was not insane, I had no problems, but she seemed to think she did. We had the same eye according to this man, but my father and grandmother never made mention of it, but they did say Sissy and I looked like her. I should have guessed at the eyes.

“Did you? Did you put her eye out?”

He shook his head, still keeping his face at a distance from me. “No, I couldn’t do that to her. Your mother was a sweet soul. I could never cause her pain, even at her request.”

“Did she come home?”

He turned further from me, my view now of the back of his head.

“Answer me! Did you bring my mother home?”

He slowly faced me. “I did,” he said in a muffled voice, his eyes concealed by the wide brim of his hat. His head hung low, his chin resting on his chest. “I brought her home, like I brought you home . . . You’re the reason I stayed on after she died. She asked me to watch over the twins. Asked me if it should start again, to put out that confounded blue eye of yours."

My stance tensed. Was this what our little talk was all about? Did he mean to cut out my eye?

"Relax Mr. Dahl, I'm not planning on laying a finger on you. No, I don't think that would help. It didn't seem to help Athena. I don't think it will help you."

"Help Athena with what? You're not making any sense."

"The evil, Sir. There's a sickness in you, there's no medicine for. It doesn't matter if you cut out your eye or keep it where it is. It runs deeper than that, much deeper. That's why I'm telling you all of this. Why I told you about your mother. Maybe I could still do right by her. Your father and grandmother have shielded you from it, sent you away as if that could fix everything, but it can't. It didn't fix your mother and it didn't fix you. I can see it in that eye of yours. I thought by you knowing the truth, well maybe, you can find your own cure." He looked past the still water of the lake to the potting shed. "Maybe that's what you were doing when you were a boy. Maybe you were trying to figure it all out. I want you to figure it out, Mr. Dahl, before it's too late. Before you join the rest of them. Just like your mother, you were so sweet. It's hard to think evil can dwell in a boy that good."

Eddy Poe came running up to me. "Kenneth! Kenneth!"

He stopped at my side. Seeing Athena's name on the cross, he raked his fingers through his brown hair. "It's true. Oh dear merciless God, it's true."

The coachman bowed, taking his leave of us. My eyes followed him.

Eddy shook my arm. "Damn it man, what happened?!" Hot tears fell from his eyes in torrents.

I felt like I woke from a dream, like my brain was still foggy from sleep. My mother had not died in childbirth, she had suffered in the sanitarium like I had, and had come home to die under the oppression of her mind. My whole life was a lie. Why would the truth be kept from me?

Eddy's tears gained momentum, mixing with whimpers that resembled an ailing dog. His countenance was one of suffering—his pallor pale, his cheeks hollowed. Welt-like bruises had settled under his already melancholy eyes. I couldn't think, not under his grief and his vice-like grip. Why was it okay for everyone else to show emotion? If I did, if I took my mask off, if only for a split second, it would be a sign of mental illness. Maybe it was Athena. Maybe it was the spell she cast on every soul that had the privilege of meeting her. Eddy was her victim as was I.

"Her heart stopped."

"Cook said she gouged out her eyes."

Slowly, almost unperceivably, I shook my head. "Rumors. It was only one eye. She died because her heart stopped."

Was I a victim of Athena or was my mother on to something? Just because my mother was mad didn't mean she couldn't be right. I had heard sane ideas come from madmen, day in and day out at Westminster. *Men [had] called me mad; but the question [was] not yet settled, whether madness is or is not the loftiest intelligence—whether much that is glorious—whether all that is profound—does not spring from disease of thought.* Was it possible Athena was *my* victim?

I marched off toward the potting shed. Eddy ran after me. "What?! Wait! Where are you going?"

The old potting shed wasn't far from the cemetery. I arrived at it so quickly, it was as if I flew. The potting shed had been abandoned before I was born for a more practical one adjacent to the solarium. It had sat untouched for nearly a decade before I'd visited it as a child, before I made it my lab. It was as I remembered it. I had spent a lot of time under its moss encrusted cedar roof before I was sent away. The stone walls were the same stones used in the construction of the servant dining hall and the family vault. They didn't bother me then, but they did now. Enough so, to make me hesitate my next move.

Back then I didn't remember falling down the steps of The Vault. However, I had recalled my past and had lived through being restrained against my will and thrown in a sanitarium for my own good. But I had nothing to fear. The walls were just small stones—hunks of earth. I was not going to let unbridled fear stand in my way. I was not a slave to the A E I O U's of insanity.

The potting shed had been boarded up after I was sent away. Wooden planks were nailed across the door in the same lazy manner as the Burnt Wing. I kicked the door open. It opened with a swoosh, the planks falling to the ground in front of the threshold. Stale air struck me in the face. I took a step back, gasping for fresh air and stepped on Eddy's shoes. Before it was a potting shed the building had been used to hold ammunition during the war and still reeked of iron.

"What are you looking for?" Eddy asked, seizing my arm again, tears stains streaking his cheeks.

I stormed in. Pulling my arm free, I shielded my nose and mouth with my hand that still clutched the bouquet of primroses. "Where are they all?"

"What?"

"You know what Eddy," I said sharply. "You're the one who followed me here."

"All of the cats have been buried, Ken."

"Pluto?"

He nodded. "Buried."

I rested on a wooden bench that had served as my dissecting

table.

"Ken, what's going on?"

"Eddy . . . Oh Eddy, I think I killed Athena. I think I influenced her to take out her eye."

He took a seat next to me on the bench. It wobbled under our weight. "I thought you said that was a rumor?"

I put up my hand, to stop his questions. "I put the idea in her head, asked her to do it. At first, she said no, like any sane, logical person would. But then my sickness crept into her—this evil—and she did it, she scooped it out with my teaspoon."

"You said her heart stopped. I'm not quite following you. Start at the beginning." His words were rushed, not following the cadence of his usual confidence. He appeared desperate to know what happened to Athena—to my Athena.

"That's true. The doctor said her heart stopped. But it's also true she gouged out one of her eyes. It was only one eye." I buried my face in my hand. "Oh Eddy, I told her I wanted her to look like me. Could you imagine wanting to change one hair on her head? But I did. In my anger, I wanted her to have one blue eye and one black void." I looked at him through splayed fingers. "I influenced her with this evil pale-blue eye of mine, just like I influenced that doctor at the sanitarium to kill himself."

Eddy's posture became rigid. He reminded me of a cat, how their eyes and ears slant to the side when they perceive a threat.

"What doctor, Ken?"

"Dr. Tarri. He deserved it. You will have to believe me when I say that." I shook my head. "But Athena—I wished I would've known. I wished the coachman would have told me on the way to Westminster everything he knew about my mother—everything she'd told him. Maybe my sweet goddess could've been spared . . . My father knew too, didn't he? He asked if I had anything to do with Dr. Tarri's death. I didn't realize until now I did."

Eddy's bloodshot eyes combed over me. The bruises under his eyes took the shape of dark crescents. I knew he didn't understand. How could he? He wasn't a Dahl. Nonetheless, I wanted his opinion. Phrenology, by way of his expansive forehead, proved he was a great intellect. If he saw evil in me, I'd know the empirical truth.

"Do you think my mother was right? Do you think it's possible I can influence people?"

"No Ken, I don't think you can, not in the way you're implying. No man can."

"My eye," I said, pushing my eyelid up so he could get a clear view of it, "do you find it unsettling?"

He laughed. It was his usual good-natured laugh, there was no jest in it. "Well yes, as a matter of course, I do. But that's simply because it's a variant of normal. What we are not used to is always queer. Strangeness doesn't possess power. I don't believe that. I'm too logical a man to believe in phantasmata and so are you. Your eyes evoke the same response as seeing a man come back from war with a missing limb. You're going to look because it's different. It's human nature to look and to feel something. In the case of the man with the missing limb, maybe it's respect, maybe it's pity. When someone looks at your eyes, I imagine they feel one thing or another and that's natural. It's to be expected, they draw such a striking comparison to each other." He put his hand on mine. "Don't let Athena's death be the reason you lose grip on reality. The last thing you want is to be sent away again."

I inhaled slowly. The cold air in my lungs helped to clear my mind. "You're right about one thing. I don't want to be sent away again. I'll take my own life before I let my father drag me back to that torture chamber. You have a choice dear Eddy: you can be a friend to me as you were a long time ago, or you can betray me again and run and tell my father everything I've just said."

He squeezed my hand. "I had no choice but to tell your father what I saw. You know that. I know you do. You are and will forever remain my dearest friend. I would do anything for you and that's why I got you help. Tell me you understand that?"

"Oh Eddy, you never understood me."

CHAPTER TWENTY-TWO

The Birthday Masquerade

I pulled out my pocket watch for what felt like the hundredth time. I put it to my ear, to make sure it was still working properly. It ticked as steady as death beetles in the walls. The small hand moved around the large hand in a steady rhythmic motion. No—there was nothing wrong with my watch. The party started an hour ago and still no guests had arrived.

My father sat in his usual seat at the head of the table in the dining hall, my grandmother in hers, and me in mine, facing the captured unicorn in the medieval tapestry. We looked more like funeral mourners than revelers dressed in all black attire and frowns. I wished we could replace some of the time worn pieces in the house, but everything was a keepsake, a precious piece of the Dahl legacy. I believed the unicorn wouldn't look so sad, his release so hopeless, if the grass was a little greener.

I ran my hand over my white opal mask that rested on the table. Its features were smoothed as if blunted by wax. I chose this particular mask because it was androgynous and lacked human expression. It was the closest mask I could find to my true face. The way I saw it, I wore a mask every day. I wanted the mask I wore for my eighteenth birthday to be my true face.

Androgynous, non-human—a mere collection of scars—emotionally handicapped—that's how they left me. That's how I saw my face in the mirror—young, almost beautiful, but irrefutably scarred.

I looked toward the stairs for a sign of Sissy. She insisted on staying in her room until the revel was in full swing, and then, and only then would she make her grand entrance.

"It must be the weather," my father said, taking a puff of his cigar.

I cursed his cigar, and I cursed him. It was the smell of his cigar that evoked the voices the night of Athena's death.

But he was right about the weather being a deterrent. It was pelting rain outside and had been that way since dawn. We had awoken to rain hitting the glass panes in loud thuds as if it was hailing, and for a little while it was. All day we heard the wind howling so loudly it sounded like human cries. The drafts caused by the high winds made it impossible to use candles, forcing all of the lamps to be lit, even in the servant quarters.

I had never seen a storm like this before. It was biblical or at least what I imagined the storms from scripture to be like. In place of the blue sky was a black one. The clouds were also black, the sun gone, barricaded by darkness. Tree branches graded the house like the claws of a hungry beast, the sashes rattled like snakes. I had assumed some people on the guest list wouldn't brave the storm, but to have not one guest show up was heartbreaking. There was no sign of Madame Prospera, and I was certain if anyone would come Hell or high water it would be her. But I suppose her flatteries were merely obligatory.

At least there was music. The musicians, coming from out of town, arrived yesterday. They were extremely talented. Particularly the violinist. He played with a passion as strong as the storm outside. The music flowed like honey into the dining hall coating us in a love ballad. My grandmother tapped her long nails on the table to the beat, she knew this song. She seemed to be having a good time now despite the lack of guests. She'd put on her mask for the party. She was a black cat, her gown solid black, matching her hair. She wore a ruby necklace that shimmered like free-flowing blood. I wondered if she did that in honor of Pluto.

An elderly servant woman, leaning heavily on her left side as a consequence of the odd shape hump on her back, came into the dining hall with another tray of food. I had watched her struggle to lift the huge silver trays all evening, but now she was right next to me, and her struggle seemed more futile. I knew as her master I should not have intervened, but I did for pity's sake.

"Let me help you," I said, going to take the tray from her.

In shock, for that's the only thing that could have explained her bizarre behavior, she dropped the tray on the ground. Little pastry puffs filled with sweet cheese, the ones that were a hit at Athena's wake, rolled across the floor.

"My dear Sir, I'm sorry," she said as she scrambled on the floor to retrieve the rolling pastries. She was on her hands and knees picking them up with a voracity that seemed superhuman.

My father let out a grunt.

"Let me help," I said, also dropping to my knees.

"I think you've helped enough Kenneth. Sit down."

I ignored my father. My fingers were already oily from the

doughy balls. The woman's hunchback prevented her from reaching the ones that rolled under the table.

I noticed the woman was trembling. "Are you ill?" I asked concerned.

"No Sir . . . it's just . . . it's just . . ."

"Just what?"

She spoke in a whisper as not to have my father hear. "She warned me not to look at it, but I did, and I'm sorry."

I stood, wiping the grease from my hands off on a cloth napkin. I knew she was talking about my eye. She was never going to be able to replace Athena, but now I knew, and I think she did too, that she would never cut it at Dahl House. "I think you should take the rest of the night off. I'll return the tray to the kitchen for you."

"That's a good idea," my grandmother said. "Kenneth's right, take the rest of the night off."

The servant woman scampered off, leaving the tray with me.

I entered the kitchen, the pocket doors to the servant dining area were open. The dining hall was armed with over two dozen servants ready to serve the guests when they arrived. Upon seeing me they stood at attention. One rushed to me to take the tray. "They fell on the floor."

Cook broke away from the stove to see what brought me into the kitchen. "What a shame," she said, examining the soiled pastries to see if they were still servable. She picked a piece of hair off one letting the stray hair fall to the ground. She blew on another to remove dirt before placing it back on the silver tray.

"Yes, it is a shame. Athena's replacement, though she was warned not to look at my eye, did. And this was the result."

Everyone's eyes darted to the ground. Apparently, everyone warned the newcomer about my eye. I'm not sure why this nettled me as it did. I knew people shied away from it. But it infuriated me. I could feel my temper growing—feel my cheeks flushing with anger. Maybe it was because this woman was Athena's replacement and Athena had looked me in that strange blue eye of mine and loved me. Maybe my eye *was* an evil eye like my mother had told the coachman or maybe it was just a variant of normal like Eddy had said, but either way Athena had loved it.

"Don't worry Sir," Cook said, wiping her hands on her apron, ultimately deciding the fallen pastries were too dirty to eat. "I will get some more of those little buggers in the oven straight away."

"I don't think that's necessary Cook. I don't think anyone is coming. My father's right, it must be the weather."

The porter, who had been sitting still on a stool by the fireplace in the servant dining hall, rose and began stoking the fire, despite the flame was burning strong. He poked at it with striking jabs as if nervous. I had gotten very good at observing people at Westminster. Reading body language had become second nature to me.

"You, Porter—those invitations I gave you, did you deliver them?"

He put the fire poker down and glanced at Cook.

"You don't answer to her, you answer to me. Did you or did you not deliver the invitations I gave you?"

He ran his hand up and down the hilt of the axe that rested near the wood pile on the side of the fireplace. He didn't do this in an egregious way as if he planned to cut me down with it, but in a nervous manner. He had to keep his hands busy and now that he had put the poker down, he was desperate. His whole body turned in on itself, which was a feat for such a brawny man.

"Uh no Sir, they were not delivered. Not a single one."

"No? Why not?"

His face flushed. "Well Sir, you did give them to me for delivering, but your father said not to. And told me to tell you if you should ask, they were delivered." His eyes diverted back to the fire. "He may have given me some coin to keep quiet about it until after the party, but uh, now that the hours upon us, I don't see the point in keeping it from you."

I tried not to show any deflection of mood. Everyone knew the party had been canceled but Sissy and me. The porter implicated the cook with his glance when I asked him about the invitations. If Cook knew, the whole household knew. They all helped to carry out my father's charade, cooking a feast and waiting in the kitchen as if guests should be arriving at any moment.

The porter glanced at me, careful not to look me in my pale-blue eye. "I'm sorry."

"I don't need your pity. Anyone's pity," I said, looking at the bowed heads of the servants. "I need your help. We have enough food to feed an army, but not one morsel has been eaten. We have a ten piece ensemble playing beautiful music in the ballroom and no one is dancing. We need revelers. All of you go to your rooms, put on your best attire, and join the party."

Cook's face lit up. "You mean it, Sir?"

"Yes, I want everyone there. Tell the entire household and make sure you tell Athena's replacement to join as well. Remember this is a masquerade birthday party so do your best to come up with a costume quickly and do hurry to make your way downstairs."

Cook seized my hand. I don't think she'd ever touched me before. Her hands were warm and moist like the pastry balls. "Oh yes Sir, right away good, kind Sir. I'll put on my very best in honor of your birthday."

"That's much appreciated. I shall see you shortly then."

I clapped my hands. "Dismissed, all of you. Get dressed."

The servants stampeded out of the kitchen. I remained there alone, thinking.

I resolved at that moment to kill my father. This party meant so much to Sissy. She had suffered so much because of me, and this party was for her. If my father thought he could take that from her and get away with it, he was dead wrong. He had to be punished—*I must not only punish but punish with impunity.*

I returned to the dining hall and took my seat at the table. I put on my mask that I'd left there. I didn't want my father to see my smile and I couldn't hide it. I would let the mask do it for me. Not even with all of Dr. Tarri's lessons, could I stop the corners of my lips from twisting into a grin.

"Well Kenneth, it looks like it's going to be an early night. Shame about the weather. But uh, I suppose we should tuck in for the evening."

My masked face inclined toward him. He sat up with a start, as if he was seeing my true face for the first time. My grin continued to twist and distort under the mask.

There was a knock at the door, his head turned toward the front entrance, not that he could see it from the dining hall. Indistinct words were exchanged with the butler. I recognized Eddy's voice. That's right, I handed him his invitation a few days ago when he'd stopped by to perform his routine check-in on me.

Eddy Poe was ushered in by the butler. "May I introduce, Mr. Edgar Allan Poe."

Out of respect, he shook my father's hand first. "Sorry, I'm late," he said, shaking my hand with his usual vigor. "The storm has really picked up. I almost didn't recognize you, that's quite a mask, a skull of sorts, I imagine?"

"Yes, I think perhaps it is," I said.

He pulled out a beaked mask he had tucked under his

elbow. "A raven," he said donning it, black feathers closing around his violet-tinted eyes like the real thing. His eyes pulled the dark color from the feathers, turning them the deep purple of a bruise. He looked around, his newly beaked face looking severe as it moved right to left. "Tell me the storm didn't keep everyone?"

Footfalls sounded on the servant staircase.

"No, not everyone. Here are the guests now."

At the sight of the servants closing around the table, my father stood. Before he could protest, I also stood, waving my hands over the food on the table. "Enjoy yourselves."

More servants nosed in. The servants worked in shifts, and on different days, so it was hard for me to get a real handle on how many servants we employed, but soon the dining hall and ballroom were swarming with life.

My father sat down and lit another cigar. "Well played Kenneth. I hope you know what you're doing."

"Yes father, I'm in perfect control of myself."

He puffed on his cigar.

Excusing myself, I went upstairs, my hand sliding up the polished banister. I walked down the carpet runner keeping my eyes on my path, paying no attention to the portraits of my ancestors that adorned the walls, their words lost in the tempest that brewed in my head.

I knocked on Sissy's bedroom door. "The party's waiting on you. I'll be waiting downstairs."

I let my finger drag down the hall, over doors and walls, stopping at Athena's door. I tapped on it lightly. Putting my lips to it I whispered, "The party's waiting on you. I'll be waiting downstairs."

I tarried by the foot of the stairs listening to the music and voices from the other rooms. Nothing was distinct, yet every sound was an important part of the party murmur. Sensing footsteps, but not hearing them, I turned to see an ocean of white satin skirts flowing down the staircase. My eyes moved upwards to see white feathered wings, and up higher to a white mask. I rushed to her with alacrity. Taking her hand, I kissed it. "Oh Athena, my angel. My sweet goddess, you've returned to me."

She pulled up her mask. A crown of dark curls spilled over it. "Kenneth, it's me."

"Sissy," I said, putting my finger through one of her curls, "of course it's you. You're my dark-haired angel."

At that moment, I thought of my father and smiled. I wondered if he would still think of me as a dark-haired angel after tonight.

Sissy giggled into her hand, "Ken, I'm not an angel. I'm a white raven."

"Eddy also came as a raven. The black variety."

She pulled down her mask, adjusting it over her petite nose.

I examined it closer. Sure enough, there was a beak, and it was adorned with small, white feathers. From the foot of the stairs, it looked smooth—a mask of Seraphim.

It dawned on me that Sissy and Eddy had coordinated outfits, but she was supposed to match me. Again, I worried she would leave me. Leave me for Eddy.

"I thought you were wearing the black dress we picked out together?"

"You look better in that dress than me, besides I wanted to surprise you. Do you like the dress?"

I rubbed a piece of her skirt between my thumb and index finger. It felt like liquid metal under my touch. The beads on the square neckline caught the light of the sconces, bringing her dress to life. Each little bead gleamed as if it were an eye. "Yes, I like it very much. It looks like Athena's dress."

She smiled. "I knew you would like this one better." Linking her arm with mine she whispered, "happy eighteenth birthday, dearest Kenneth."

I kissed her cheek. She was cold. "Happy birthday Sissy."

We entered the ballroom together. The dance floor separated for her as if Moses, himself, was parting the revelers with the divine hand of God. She got her entrance. Everyone clapped. My beautiful sister was getting the recognition she deserved. I felt so happy, everything else melted away. It was an elation I had never known. She sparkled under the glass globe chandelier that lit the room in a prismatic bubble. The brass stem was anchored to the vaulted ceiling by plaster pomegranates, apples, cherries, and grapes, clustered between folds of flowers. I smiled. I had never noticed the daisies and the violets in the ceiling medallion. Perhaps because the chandelier was so seldom lit. But there they were, daisies and violets amongst roses. Not one thorn was visible. Everything was perfect. The hand painted morning glories on the ceiling wrapped around the room bending softly around the corners, encircling my beautiful sister from high above us. She was the most vivid of the morning glories basking in the light of the ballroom chandelier.

I retreated to the nearest wall. Crowds were never my thing. From there, I watched Sissy make her way through the dance floor. She found Eddy who was feverishly writing in his pocket-size book. They really were two peas in a pod. Watching them together, as he wrote and she eagerly read his words, filled me with a sense of dread.

I was going to marry Athena and she was going to stay at Dahl House with me—with me and Sissy. But Eddy would never stay here. He aspired to be a famous writer. He would never be satisfied in our ancestral home, no matter the luxuries we could afford. What of Sissy then? Would she leave me as Athena left me? Would she—could she—leave me all alone?

"How nice of you to invite the entire household. Your father never would have invited everyone," my grandmother said, approaching me. I kept my eyes on Sissy and Eddy.

"My father's not a Dahl. I am and Sissy is. I wasn't going to let him spoil Sissy's birthday. He may want to punish me, but Sissy should not have to bear the brunt of it."

She took my hand and squeezed it. "You made Sissy proud tonight."

My eyelids fluttered down to her. Her blue eyes glistened from her mask like a cat's at night. "Thank you, Grandmama."

I sought Sissy and Eddy again, but I couldn't spot them. They were lost in the throng. The room was packed mostly with two types of servants. The servants who painted their faces white and the ones who had painted them red. With the short notice, I was surprised they were even able to come up with that. But yet, Cook was able to put together an ensemble that made it seem like she knew she would be a guest of honor. She wore a blue gown and from the crown of her head, jutted feathers. I supposed her to be a peacock. She was having a wonderful time spinning around the dance floor.

In one gesture of humility, I had done what it took four years to do at the sanitarium. Just as I had won the panel of doctors over to my side, I had won the hearts of the entire staff.

Tonight, we were equals, enjoying a party together they would only ever have been spectators at, and for that, they gave me their loyalty.

My father reveled with them. His squat appearance and brown mask made me think of an ape. He'd already shown that consorting with servants wasn't below him. He had forced Athena into an affair with him, but they, like her, did not like him. In contrast, every servant who passed me tilted their hat or inclined their head toward me and I saw a gleam in their eyes. It was the same thing I noticed in my own eyes as love for Athena. They loved me. They didn't love me because they understood me. It was not the love I desired from an intimate. They loved me for treating them as equals and in that was power.

I noticed a tall and slender woman with long, dark hair. She wore a solid black mask that hid her entire face, and the black dress Sissy was originally going to wear tonight. I was certain of it. It was the same dress we had tried on at Madame Prospera's together. It had the same sweeping neckline, the same full skirt.

Did Sissy change her dress? . . . No—there she was with Eddy wearing Athena's dress. No—that wasn't right. Athena was buried in that dress. It was just one that looked like hers.

I left my grandmother's side and approached the woman. She moved further and further from me. I weaved around servants. I noticed the white-faced servants all had dark crescents under their eyes as if they were all meant to be skeletons. Their makeup was fantastical, with dark shadows hollowing out their cheekbones. The red-faced servants were gruesome. Their faces were made up of patches of red and raw flesh as if burnt. Their eyes peered from their blood masks like marbles. I pushed my way through them, following the dark-haired woman into the hall.

I grabbed her hand, forcing her to stop. "Wait, please. Who are you? Where did you get that dress?" She turned to me, not saying a word. Her mask was as smooth as black opal and androgynous as my own. Her dark, straight hair encircled her mask, blending in with it. I could only make out her one eye, a very pale-blue eye. I knew that eye. I pushed up her mask to see my face. It was the face I had become so familiar with in the cellar's mercury mirror. It was right before me. There was my sloping nose, my mismatched eyes, my chiseled chin. I reached out and touched my face, realizing I was touching my portrait.

This was my new portrait—painted and hung in anticipation of my eighteenth birthday. It hung next to Sissy's portrait. She was still a little girl in the painting. I wondered why her new portrait wasn't hung up. I could feel the moisture under my fingertips, the paint was still tacky on my portrait. The rainy weather must have kept it from drying. I dug my nails into the painting, peeling back the paint. Behind my portrait was another painting that had been painted over. The face looked a lot like mine, but the chin was the gentle chin of a woman. It was not unlike Sissy's small, bantam jawline. I took the oval portrait off the wall. I popped it out of its gold gilt frame to see if there was a name or artist's insignia on the back of it.

"That's the only portrait of your mother," the coachman said, from behind me.

"That's her?" I turned the portrait around, scrutinizing it—seeing all the ways my mother and I were alike, and there were many. If it wasn't for the jaw line, this portrait could have been of me.

"Why would my father have her painted over?"

When the coachman didn't answer, I pulled my eyes away from the portrait. He was gone.

I nibbled on the inside of my lip. I was losing it. Was the coachman just there or . . . or was he in my head. The woman in the black dress, she was clearly not there. She was an illusion. Illusion was one of the cardinal vowels of insanity, but I wasn't insane.

I rushed down the steps to the kitchen, knowing no one would be in there. I fumbled for the matches in my pocket. I needed clarity. I needed to know what I saw was real. I shoved two matchsticks under my already sore nailbeds, breaking them off at the nail. The pain felt good. Damnit, I needed more. With great effort, I jammed one under my thumbnail.

"That's not what you need Sir, if you don't mind me saying it."

I turned to see the coachman. I hid my hand behind my back.

"Hiding the truth never helped anyone. That's exactly what your father's been trying to do all these years. Don't hide."

"I'm not hiding," I said. "I just need clarity. The pain helps me to focus. It shuts everything else out."

"It's your choice Mr. Dahl."

"Wait, what aren't you telling me?"

I followed him into the hall, but he was gone. In fact, most of the revelers were. The party was winding down. The musicians had broken down their instruments and were heading to the rooms prepared for them. I didn't realize I had been away for that long. A few stragglers stumbled out of the ballroom, drunk on champagne and Amontillado.

Sissy sat with Eddy on a settee placed against the wall. They looked so small in the space. Eddy was still writing in his book and Sissy in hers.

I approached them, peering over their works. Sissy was still struggling with her writer's block and despite me telling her the correct way to spell damn, went on misspelling it, dropping the letter 'N'.

Becoming aware of my presence, Eddy quickly closed his book.

"Secret, is it?" I asked.

"No, of course not. It's just that it's not finished."

"What's it about?"

He pushed his beaked mask up and smiled a toothy grin. "It's about twins who share a peculiar fate."

I smiled back, returning his grin. "I'm very glad our little birthday party served as a muse. Well, don't let me stop you," I said mainly to Sissy. "I have something I have to do. I'll be back shortly."

CHAPTER TWENTY-THREE

An Axe to Grind

I made my way back into the kitchen with its worn stone floor and claustrophobic stone walls. The smells of my birthday delicacies were still thick in the air as if Cook was busy in the kitchen whipping up more. But she wasn't there—no one was there. Without dawdling, I went to the wood pile and took hold of the axe the porter had brought to my attention to earlier. It felt heavy in my hands—heavier than I'd imagined it would feel. This strengthened my conviction. Everything worth doing was hard work. If my work now was too easy, it would be wrong. "Idle hands spread the Devil's work," I muttered.

The servants had drunk and danced themselves into a stupor. The night was mine, but I was a careful man. I took the main staircase in case a few servants still lingered about. Even tonight, they took the staircases designed for staff only. Equality is repressed in the mind of the suppressed. The suppressed keep themselves there. I understood that. I was the same way. I let my father keep me beneath him, when we both knew I was his superior.

I took the steps one tread at a time. I was in no rush. Eddy and Sissy were fully engrossed. And no doubt in my absence, Eddy would stay longer. Enjoying my sister's company uninterrupted was a thing he seldom got now that I was home.

I went down the hall passing my room, Sissy's room, Athena's room, before coming to my father's. I stood outside his door for a moment looking at the cherry wood paneling. I had never stepped foot in my father's apartments.

I turned the knob slowly, careful not to let the knob let out a groan. I closed the door in the same manner.

The room was dark, the storm still raged outside, shutting out the moon and stars. Detection was not a concern. His breathing was deafening. He inhaled and exhaled in gulps like he was a fish out of water.

I waited for my eyes to adjust before making my way to the center of the room. My father's bed was situated between two tall windows and flanked by side tables. In front of the window to the left, with an excellent view of the tarn, was a wingback chair and a writing desk. His room had a very similar layout to mine—his being grandiose.

I approached the bed. My father was on his back. Yes, I could see the rise and fall of his chest. There was no need to light a candle, I saw what I needed to. I placed the axe on the side of the chair and disrobed. I neatly folded my clothes and placed them on the seat of the chair.

Once naked, I picked the axe up again, examining the blade. It was dull, marred with scratches. It was perfect.

The up and down of his enormous stomach under his navy

sheets reminded me of rolling waves, his snoring symbolic of the storm soon approaching. I raised the axe over my head. No—this was too good for him. Dying in his sleep was too peaceful a way to go. I wanted him to know it was me who killed him—killed him for sending me to the sanitarium—killed him for letting Dr. Tarri do what he did to me—killed him for touching Athena, but foremost— killed him for hurting Sissy.

"Father," I said in a calm whisper. For I was not angry, but calm. Anger was the first of Dr. Tarri's cardinal vows of insanity. And there was no man on Earth as calm as me. "Father." His eyelids twitched. He was coming to. "Oh Father," I said melodically, my voice louder.

He opened his eyes. I waited for him to realize what was about to happen. I couldn't rush this. I waited for his eyes to adjust to the darkness as mine had. I wanted him to see my face, the face of his only son, standing over him with an axe. I wanted him to fear, for as I had learned long ago—*never to suffer would never to have been blessed.* This was my parting gift to my father.

I was in control—in perfect control, my pulse steady, my breathing even. Once I saw the terror in his face—saw his pupils dilate to the size of black pennies, I brought the axe down splitting his skull.

"I see a problem and I fix it."

A splash of cool blood splattered across my face and chest. *Blood was [my] Avatar.* It felt refreshing on my hot skin—a life giving balm. With the inside of my elbow, I wiped my face, getting a better look. Tears of happiness welled in my eyes. My suppressor and the suppressor of my sister, the outsider, was dead—and I had killed him.

I pulled the axe from his skull, a sucking noise released with the pressure of the blade. I placed the bloody axe over his chest as if it had been his sword in life and he had died heroically at battle. For in the end, he *did* die for what he believed in. He died because he thought I was mad and sent me away. He'd regret that now if he could. It was a pity we *never could* get on the same page.

I cleaned my hands on the bedsheets before I took the matchbox from my pants and lit a candle. I went to my father's washstand and cleansed my hands, chest, and face as well as I could with his small shaving mirror. The water in the bowl soon became pink with my spoils.

Looking at myself in my father's private mirror felt empowering. I examined my face for a long time after it was free of blood. I wished I could relive this moment over and over again and remember how good I felt—how free.

I toweled my face and chest dry and went to the chair to get my clothes. Standing at the foot of my father's bed was my grandmother. My body stiffened, not in embarrassment for her seeing me naked, but in fear of what she was going to do. Would she scream for help?

The axe was too far away. She would scream before I could silence her. With most of the household intoxicated, her cry for help may go unnoticed, but maybe it wouldn't. I fell back into my role of the suppressed. I would let her decide my fate.

We both remained as still as statues. I didn't move to cover myself. I was no longer bashful about my own nakedness; the sanitarium, in the end, had helped me overcome that.

There was silence between us for a long time before she spoke. "He's dead," she finally said.

"Yes, he's dead. I killed him."

"Get dressed Kenneth. We have to get rid of the body before anyone sees it."

I put on my pants, keeping my eyes on my grandmother.

She was still in her gown from the masquerade. She'd pushed her cat mask onto her forehead. It acted as a headband pulling back her dark mane. I couldn't see her eyes in the dark room, only a sliver of a glare could be detected on her glasses.

I put my mask back on, pushing it to my forehead like hers. "We'll hide your father's body in The Vault."

I had not thought about what to do with my father's body after I killed him. But the conclusion was obvious, there was only one place to conceal the body. No one goes to the family vault, and no one would smell my father's decomposing corpse in the belly of Dahl House. I would take the key to the gate to make sure of it.

I nodded, preparing my father's corpse to be moved. His blood smelled sweet to me. This must be the smell of victory.

I wrapped a towel around his head to soak up the blood. It was amazing to see the many layers under the human face. It was like a flower blooming. I wondered if Athena would like this type of flower. I wish I had more time to pull back the petals and see what made my father, my father, but I felt the weight of my grandmother's stare—I was taking too long.

My attention diverted again. I noticed Athena's book on roses rested on my father's bedside table. I opened it to see the bookmark I had given her. I touched it, feeling closer to her. The violets, a symbol of wisdom and a symbol of my Pallas Athena, gave me hope as violets also symbolize hope, that I would see her again. I took the bookmark, tucking it in my inside jacket pocket. I placed the book back on the table. He had bartered for that book. He got the book, I got to keep my long hair. Let it be forgotten like him.

Back on task, I rolled my father up like an insect in a spider's web with his own sheets and duvet cover. My grandmother helped me lower my burden to the ground. I took the wrapped bundle by the feet and dragged it to the door.

We made our way to the catacombs below the house slowly and with care not to make too much noise. We used the main staircase, assuming there was less risk of being seen on this route, much as I had decided when I had made my way up it with the axe. It would take longer this way, but it was a necessary precaution.

Right before my father's head would drop to the next stair tread, I'd circle back around, and with my hands place his head on the next tread so it wouldn't thud. We traveled this way until we got to the Burnt Wing. I moved swiftly now, the fear of being heard nonapplicable. I knew, all too well, no one besides me came this deep into the house.

We made it to the gate of the family vault. The iron ravens, for now I knew them to be the corvids of transformation and not crows, greedily looked down on us as if our offering of flesh was not enough. Their beaks were hungry. My grandmother unlocked the gate, not giving stock to the birds, but I couldn't help staring at their beady black eyes and seeing the hunger within them. I don't think the hunger they suffered from could be satiated. From their perch amongst the berries and leaves, they were the minions of Death. The gatherers of the dead. My father's keepers.

My grandmother swung the gate open and moved ahead of me with a lantern to light the way. I did not fear the catacombs with her, it felt natural following her in this way. I dragged my father's lifeless body down the old staircase, each tread sounding with a dull thud. Each thud resonated louder and longer the deeper into the catacombs we went. The stoney walls acted as a sound amplifier, keeping the echoes trapped in the dark with us.

We made it to the foot of the stairs, the smell of smoke clinging to my nostrils. I wiped the beads of sweat from my temple with the back of my hand. "Maybe I should drag him into one of the niches behind the stairs in case there's an investigation," I suggested.

My grandmother approached the cherub carved platform in the center of the crypt. "I have a better place."

I didn't like the idea of placing my father's corpse in the marble coffin Athena's body had recently rested in, but reasoned hiding him in plain sight was, in fact, a good hiding spot. I dragged my father's corpse to the platform.

With her index finger, my grandmother pushed a small button camouflaged as a cherub's eye. The top of the platform, including the open marble coffin on it, slid aside with a loud grating noise revealing a hidden compartment.

Stale air and the stench of decay wafted from it. I covered my nose and mouth with the palm of my hand. Interred in the platform was a corpse. "Who is this?" I muttered, taking the lantern from my grandmother and examining the body. The lantern burned stronger than five candles and I saw the corpse in explicit detail. The body was mummified, dried and withered to a flaky charcoal tone. Its once light dress was dappled in dirt with little specks of fungi that shone in the darkness like fireflies. The corpse's long, dark hair coiled around the face and shoulders like pythons. The eyelids had shriveled, curling backward away from the eyes, one dark eye dried like the pit of a fruit, the other eye was missing.

My pulse elevated. I felt a surge in my chest. There were deep grooves scratched into the lid of the marble platform and the sides of it. I knew at once this woman was placed in this tomb alive. It was the faceless woman. The woman in white. The blacked out face I saw was the reflection of the inside of her tomb. She'd clawed at her tomb until the lid was a collection of deep scars seen on her apparition. In vain, she'd attempted to free herself with the brute force of her fingernails. The mummified corpse's nails were slit and worn, the fingers broken and contorted from their failed labor. In her one hand, squeezed amongst the misshapen, withered fingerbones was Athena's beautiful, blue eye that had never been found. It was oozing and raw in distinct comparison to the mummified, claw-like hand.

"We should put your father with your mother."

"My mother?" I asked, glancing back at my grandmother before returning my focus to the corpse. "So it's true, the faceless woman was my mother. . . "

I fought the flood of tears that stung the back of my throat. Emotion is a cardinal vowel of insanity and I had been epically stoic this whole time. I didn't want to give off the picture of insanity standing next to my father's mutilated corpse. I wanted my grandmother to know I killed him with a sane mind.

With a lowered voice, not wanting it to echo in the vast space I said, "This is it then, how she really died? My mother was brought home from the sanitarium to only be imprisoned somewhere just as bad."

"We had no choice, Kenneth."

"We?"

"Your father and I."

Despite my best effort, my voice shook. "You were a part of it?. . . You had no choice but to sentence my mother to a premature burial? What gave you the right?"

"You must understand, we did all we could for her. We sent her to the sanitarium trying to get her the help she needed. We funded the research, brought in the best doctors. She fooled them all and returned home more disturbed than when she left us."

She buried her face in her one hand, the cat mask staring at me from atop her head. "She, like you and Sissy, had one blue eye and one brown eye. She was obsessed with her blue eye. At first, she thought it was evil—"

I finished my grandmother's sentence. "Thought it let her know things and do things."

"Yes, but these things Ken, they were all in her head. She too heard voices, like you did."

I refrained from telling her I still do.

"We tried to appease her. A priest came to live at Dahl House. That worked for a while until it didn't. Where religion failed, we thought science would prevail. We sent her to the sanitarium. She spent nearly six years there. Thinking her cured, she was released and came home. That first night home, she clawed out her blue eye with her fingernails."

I glanced at the mummified corpse of my mother, at the vacant eye socket.

"Her body recovered in time, but her mind never did. The eye she thought was evil was gone, but now that it was, she couldn't live without it. She began to obsess over other people's blue eyes."

My grandmother took off her glasses and stepped closer to me, her tired face highlighted in the bright light of the lantern. She popped out her glass eye. In my bewilderment, I stared at it cupped in her palm.

"Your mother scooped out my eye when I was asleep."

"What?! No—my mother would never have done that. My mother was good and kindhearted. My mother was—"

"She was insane, Kenneth. She was my daughter and I loved her, but she was insane."

Tears hit my cheeks. They were not refreshing like my father's blood. They stung, their literal betrayal too keenly felt as they rolled down my face. "So that's how you dealt with her. You buried her alive?" I asked, pointing to my mother's corpse.

"No Ken." She pushed her glass eye into her empty socket and put her glasses back on. "But we did lock her away in The

Vault. For many years she lived below Dahl House undisturbed. Her meals were taken to her once a day by your father or me. The servants thought she was sent back to the sanitarium and died there. And we had told Sissy and you she had died long before that."

"That's why there's a lock on the gate. It was to keep my mother in."

My grandmother took a step away from me. Her face now bathed in shadows. "Do you remember sneaking into The Vault with Sissy when you were a boy?"

I pawed at my tears. "Yes. I remember falling down the stairs and hitting my head."

"You didn't fall Kenneth. You were pushed. Your mother pushed you down the stairs that day."

I understood only a fraction of what my mother must have endured at the sanitarium and in the family vault. But there was no way she meant to push me that day. She knew who I was. She knew my name. I remember her calling it to me in her soft voice. Surely, she wouldn't want to hurt her own son.

"The voice I heard . . ."

"Yes Ken, that was your mother's voice you heard that day. You had heard her, but after you woke up from your coma you said you still could. But that wasn't possible. Your mother had died before you regained consciousness. She started the fire of 1821 that killed all those servants and my brother. It came from below the house. We assumed she must have used the candle and matches she procured from Sissy and you to light it. We always thought she perished in the fire, assuming her body turned to ash under the heat. But now I know what really happened. She climbed into the hidden crypt, most likely thinking she could survive the fire in the cool marble until the fire burnt through the catacombs, but the inside spring mechanism must have malfunctioned trapping her. I didn't know she knew about the secret button, I never thought to check for her in there."

She took her glasses off to wipe tears. "So, you see Kenneth, there's no way you heard your mother's voice after the day you fell. I hoped you would get better, but when you didn't, and things escalated in the potting shed the way they did, I had no choice but to send you away."

My heart and my head throbbed. "It was you who sent me to Westminster?"

"Yes, it was me. Your father didn't think the sanitarium could help you since it didn't help your mother, but we had invested so much time and money into groundbreaking science, I knew if they couldn't help you no one could. I had to try. As hard as it was for me to send you away, the sanitarium was my only hope of getting my sweet grandson back. Ken, you've done the impossible. You've suffered a severe head injury most doctors thought you would never wake up from. You impressed the doctors at the sanitarium with your progress. You've come so far, and I thought it was all over when you came home, but then Athena was found murdered."

She sniffled, wiping a tear from under her glasses with her thumb.

"I didn't do that to Athena, Grandmama."

"Kenneth, my sweet grandson, we both know you did. But it's not your fault. You're sick."

"No," I said, shaking my head virulently, taking a step back. "I loved Athena. Nay—I love her. I will always love her. I would never hurt her. I just asked her to prove her love for me. And I only did it," I said, pointing at my father's corpse, "because she betrayed me because of him. I never would have asked Athena to put her eye out if it wasn't for him!"

I held the lantern over my mother's corpse. "See, here's proof I didn't kill Athena, my mother did! She has her eye in her hand. I know it's Athena's. I know her eyes anywhere."

"Kenneth, your mother's dead. She can't hurt anyone."

I spoke hurriedly. *"In the deepest slumber—no! In delirium—no! In a swoon—no! In death—no! Even in the grave all is not lost!* I've seen her. I've seen her down here and I've seen her in the sitting room." I glanced at the bundled corpse on the ground. "Father has seen her too."

"Ken, there was only one other person who knew about the secret button, and that's you. When you were very young, and your mother was in the sanitarium, you used to accompany me to the cellar. You liked looking at your reflection in the mirror in the bathroom with the daisy wallpaper. I'd take you to the chapel and sometimes I'd take you into the catacombs and tell you family stories. I would even let you climb inside the cherub platform to play."

I shook my head, silent tears falling.

"When you came home, you must have found your mother's corpse. Your father suspected you were coming down here. I had failed to see the harm in it, but now I do. It wasn't your mother who went into Athena's room and scared her to death—it was you. You saw your mother had an eye missing and you took that poor girl's eye out to give to her. You always took pride in knowing you looked like your mother and took pride in fixing things. You were always my little helper. I guess, this was your way of fixing your mother."

I leaned on the platform, my legs like noodles. "Grandmama no, that's not right. I wouldn't do that. I've never hurt anyone." My body shook as if I suffered from convulsions. I placed the lantern on the edge of the marble platform before I dropped it and started another fire.

I *had* hurt someone. I had put an axe through my father's skull.

My voice trembled like my body. "I wouldn't hurt Athena, she was to be my wife. You found Athena's eye and placed it there. I had no idea the platform opened. But you did. You never showed me how it worked."

"I love you Kenneth, more than anyone in my life, I have loved you, but this has gone far enough. I tried to help you, but after seeing what you did to your father, I know there's no helping you. What I'm doing is mercy."

She pulled out a pistol she had tucked away in her gown and pointed it at my chest. I recognized it as one of my father's dueling pistols. She must have taken it when we were in his room. I studied her, the way her tears flowed asymmetrically, how the pistol shook in between her hands.

"I don't understand. I killed my father for Sissy. He was a bad man."

She shook her head. "No Kenneth, you're the bad man."

My mother's voice whispered to me. "Ask her why she was in your father's room tonight."

I felt revigorated. My calm and confidence returned tenfold. I solved this puzzle. The corner of my lip curled into a smirk. "I see what this is. You sent my mother away convincing her she was crazy, all so you could carry on an affair with my father. That's why you were in his room tonight, wasn't it? You were visiting your lover and happened to find me."

Before she could deny it, I waved my hand dismissively. "The voices told me. Your own daughter told me. In Athena's hand I found dark hair. It was your hair. You took out Athena's eye. You killed her because you were jealous of her. You knew she was carrying on an affair with your lover and you put an end to it. I know I would never hurt Athena and furthermore I didn't know where her room was. But you did Grandmama. You were the only one that didn't rush out of their room when Cook found Athena's body and screamed bloody murder. There was no need, you already knew what happened, you were her murderess.

"You solved one problem, so you moved onto the next one. You placed Athena's eye with my mother's corpse all so you could try to convince me I was insane. You knew her corpse was hidden in the platform because you buried her alive in there after she came home from the sanitarium. That's right, I remember—my mother was already dead when I fell down the steps. I didn't see her, but her apparition. My mother didn't start the fire of 1821, you did, to kill your brother. You wanted full control of the family fortune. Giving my father executive rights wasn't enough, you needed reassurance your twin wouldn't become well again and regain control of the fortune."

The pistol weighed down my grandmother's hands. With great effort she attempted to steady it, but it was kinetic, shifting right to left like she was shooting at a moving target. But I didn't move. *I smiled—for what had I to fear?* I did nothing wrong. I was sane.

"This is all part of your little scheme to ship me off to another insane asylum and keep control of the family fortune. Well, I'm sorry to disappoint you Grandmama, but I am not insane and not you or anyone else can convince me of that. I am in full control of my actions. I killed my father, but I am not going to kill you. You sent my mother and me to the sanitarium, locked us away like rats in a cage and that's precisely what I'm going to do to you. I will keep you locked down here for the rest of your life like you sought to do with my mother."

"I love you Kenneth," she said as she applied pressure to

the trigger.

Nothing happened, the pistol jammed. I walked toward her with meaningful strides and took the pistol from her, tossing it into the blinding darkness of the catacombs. I pulled the matchbox from my pants pocket and handed it to my grandmother. "Let's see if history repeats itself."

Turning from her, I took the lantern and headed toward the stairs, the mineral deposits on the wall pulling the color from the flame until the walls were blanketed in a rutty red like dripping blood.

My grandmother chased after me. "You can't leave me down here Kenneth!" She clung to my leg, attempting to stop my ascent. I shook her off. She fell to her knees, pounding on the stone floor with her knuckles. It sounded like the muffled beat of my father's heart right before the axe struck his skull. "You can't leave me down here alone!"

From the top of the stairs, I called down to her. "I'm not. You're with your lover and your daughter."

CHAPTER TWENTY-FOUR

Stars Apart

I felt nothing, hollowed out. My grandmother was not who I believed her to be. Her sobs were barely audible from the other side of the gate. She cried for herself, not for me. But that didn't matter. No one would hear her, and the adorning ravens didn't seem to care. I put the key to the gate lock in my pants pocket, there was no leaving the family vault now. Her fate and her tomb were sealed. Her only transformation would be to dust.

I had no concept of time. I was unsure how long ago I'd left Sissy with Eddy in the ballroom or if they would still be there. I promptly made my way back to the main part of the house. It was somehow quieter as if the house itself slumbered. There were no sounds of the house settling, no moaning of the floorboards, no sound of the gas hissing as it fed the sconces—there was more life in the catacombs.

I made it to the ground floor and was about to pass the entrance when I saw Eddy with Sissy. There was no sign of the doorman, he must have gone to sleep. They lingered by the front door talking in whispers. Their contrasting white and black outfits matched the marble and black granite checkered floor they gracefully stood upon.

They looked like the king and queen of a chessboard. They looked like they belonged there and belonged together. Where did I fit into this game? What piece was I to play? A rook? A knight? To Eddy, I was a pawn—disposable. But he didn't dispose of me. I was back and I was never leaving Dahl House.

Sissy's soft mouth traveled from his cheek to his lips. I would check the queen for her own good. I abruptly interrupted. "Leaving without saying goodbye?"

Eddy turned to me, extending his hand. "Oh, there you are, I thought you'd forgotten all about me and went off to bed."

I shook his hand, with more vigor than my usual indifference. I was the man of the house now after all. "No Eddy, I'm a trustworthy friend, if I say I'll be back, then I'll be back."

He shook my hand again. "Happy Birthday ole' boy."

I opened the large, lacquered door for him, not bothering to insist he stayed the night by reason of the late hour. I didn't want him in the same house as my sister. He stepped out into an unexpectedly calm night. The storm had passed and took with it all of the clouds. It was still the middle of the night, but the sky took on twilight's golds with the richness of twinkling stars and a full moon.

Eddy waved from the bottom of the stairs. Following suit, I gave a slight wave before closing the door to the night and to Eddy Poe.

"Well," I said, turning to my sister, "I hope you had a happy birthday."

"I did thanks to you. But our birthday is not over yet." She pointed to a small box on the marble credenza in the foyer. "Happy Birthday, darling Kenneth."

I picked up the small box with a smile. Having no inclination of what I was to find inside, I unwrapped the brown paper with a schoolboy's heart. I let the paper fall to the floor, captivated by my reflection in the small mirror at the bottom of the box.

"It's a pin," she said, running her delicate finger around the braided silver frame. "I thought you should have your own mirror. I don't see the harm it could do. It's just a little one."

"I have a very similar pin," I said, mesmerized by the coincidence of it. It looked so much like the one Athena had given me. I was just about to flip open the back and look for her name when Sissy pinned it to my lapel.

"There, that's what you've been missing all night. She pulled down my mask. Now we're ready for a ball!" She took both of my hands, spinning me around in a circle like she used to when we were children.

I laughed out loud. She could be so whimsical. Everything appeared entirely different and yet the same as we spun around the room. Things I thought I knew blurred into each other, distorting truths, making their own reality. I wondered if that was how it was for the insane. 'Perception is a powerful device.'

Sissy's white raven mask took on the appearance of a skull, her body seeming to stretch out taller, larger. Her hair—longer, straighter, darker.

She spun me around until I begged her to stop.

Leaning against the wall, I waited for the room to stop spinning. "I have something for you too. Well, it's more of a something I want to share with you. Will you come?"

"Of course," she said, locking arms with me, her equilibrium restored before mine was.

We walked the same path we took as children. Soon we stood before the entrance to the Burnt Wing. The scent of smoke wafted from its corridors like phantoms from the past.

It came to my attention that the chapel's stained-glass window which marked the terminus of the wing's main hall had suffered another fracture. The main crack had spider webbed over Christ's extremities like a poison. It wouldn't be long now, pieces of his body would come crashing down to earth like the chapel, returning to dust *in sure and certain hope of the Resurrection to eternal life.*

The new crack, as straight as an arrow, traveled through the stained-glass window of the crucified Christ and down the middle of my family's crest, through the sun and the helmet of the knight. A piece had fallen from the granite keystone. Under the knight's helmet a bit of skull was visible. Yes, under the Dahl knight's helmet was a fleshless skull. I would not take this as a sign of death or mortality, but a sign of Dahl perseverance and toughness. Yes, Dahls always persevere, and I am a Dahl.

I turned to Sissy, whose eyes were on the fractured family crest. "Do you remember coming down here with me before I was sent away?"

"Yes."

I helped her maneuver under the nailed wooden boards, making sure her dress didn't get snagged. It would be a shame to ruin such an angelic dress.

It wasn't long before we stood in front of the cellar bathroom door. "I remember there was a bathroom behind this door," she said. "I'd forgotten all about it."

I swung open the door, bringing her into the small bathroom. With my foot, I softly closed the door behind us. I wasted no time lighting the candle sitting on the ledge of the crawl space window with the matches I had left there. The air in the bathroom was hot and humid, thanks to the house's many fireplaces having been lit due to the storm, but I didn't mind. My sister's perfume purified the intimate space. I was recalled to the smell of the daisies on the wallpaper, the very first time I'd smelled them. Nothing could have smelled better.

I turned Sissy around to face the mirror. I stood behind her. "I wanted to share the mirror with you."

She was about to scold me for having a mirror when she laughed, half turning to flick the oval mirror pinned to my lapel. Her laugh filled the small space, her little hiccups of happiness filling my heart with song.

"Do you see the stars in the mirror?" I asked, leaning forward to whisper it in her ear. "They're so clear tonight." The smell of daisies was palpable now—so real now. It was as if she wore a daisy chain in her hair. I wished I had brought Athena here, showed her my mirror, let her share in our starry reflection.

Sissy gazed into the mirror. "No, I only see us."

"Look closer," I said, pressing her to the sink. I untied her mask and then untied my own, letting them fall to the floor. "There's thousands of little stars trapped in the mirror."

She went to touch the mirror; I guided her hand back to her side. "No," I whispered in her ear from behind her, closer than I had been before. "You mustn't touch it."

"Why?" she asked, emulating my whisper as she continued to stare at our reflection.

"Grandmama says it will make you go mad."

She turned in my arms, the top of her head grazing my nose. "That's silly."

"Yes, it is," I said, brushing her dark hair away from her face.

"But over the last four years, there have been times I wondered . . . I wondered if she'd told me the truth. Before I returned home, I always thought I heard the voices after I'd touched it. I thought, maybe touching it *had* done something to me, changed me somehow. I thought maybe Grandmama was right, and it drove me mad.

"But I have learned—*the boundaries which divide Life from Death are at best shadowy and vague. Who shall say where the one ends, and where the other begins?* These voices came from the house at first. One was even Mother's. But the others—well, I think some came from Heaven and some I'm sure came from Hell. A little part of me has always felt special for getting to hear what the angels and demons whisper about in the dark. Oh Sissy, how they whisper."

"What do they say?"

"Sometimes I can't understand them, they're muffled or in a language foreign to me. And yet—*in snatches, [I learned] something of the wisdom which is of good, and more of the mere knowledge which is of evil.* But sometimes they are as clear as your voice. Tonight, the voices are saying we are free, and we are meant to be together—forever."

She turned back to the mirror. "I don't see stars, but I do see us. And I *know* we're meant to be together. I'm so happy you came home. I've been so lonely without you."

"Sometimes Sissy, I think you're the only one who understands me."

"I am," she said with her usual zest. "That's because we're twins. We shared the womb. Our hearts have been beating together since before we were born."

In the dim light, her white gown seemed dark. I ran my hand across her collar bone recalling how I looked in the black dress she was supposed to wear this evening.

"Do you really think I have a better chest than you?"

She turned, facing me again and smiled. "Yes, definitely, I'm as flat as a boy."

I ran my hand across her chest, her nipples between my fingers felt so soft—so good—like my grandmother's cat had felt under my caresses. I wondered how her tongue would feel on my skin. If its touch would envelop me in gooseflesh like Pluto's kisses had.

I leaned forward planting a soft kiss on her lips. Harder now—smearing her lip balm on mine, letting my thin lips move across her plump ones.

"Ken, what are you doing?" she asked, our temples touching.

I responded with another kiss, my back arching like a predator over my virtuous sister. "God, I love you." My tongue darted into her mouth, wrapping around hers until it hurt.

She placed her hands on my shoulders to separate us. She shook her head ever so slightly and spoke to me in a murmur. "Kenneth, no."

"You kissed Eddy."

"That's different."

"How so? I can accept that you love both of us. I know that's how it is, and I hate him for that. But it's an impossibility that he loves you more than I do. I have thought about you every second of every day for the last four years. Can he say that? I murdered Father tonight for you. Would Eddy have done that?"

"Father's dead?"

"Yes, I killed him because he cancelled your party. I did it for love. I love you Sissy and I want us to be together."

She took my hand, not unkindly. "This is wrong."

"The voices say it's not. They tell me we belong together, and you said it yourself—we have one heart."

"Ken, there are no voices."

Salty tears sprang to life, rolling down my cheeks. I didn't hold them back. I didn't have to in front of Sissy. "There are and I hear them," I said, my voice trembling with frustration. If only she could hear them. I pressed my lips to her hard, backing her up onto the sink. Our teeth clashed. Her back hit the mirror. The bottom corners of the mirror splintered off falling into the sink.

"I know you miss her Kenneth, but I'm not Athena."

"I know that," I said, giving distance between us. I ran my hand down her white satin dress. "But this dress . . . this dress is Athena's. I recognize it. It has to be. The dress has all of the little white beads Athena's had. It even has the blood stains on it from my finger."

I slid my hands under her skirts. "You're a white raven tonight. Ravens signify transformation. Why can't you be Sissy and Athena? Tonight, you're my angel goddess and my dark-haired angel."

She pushed my hands off of her cold thighs. I picked the broken pieces of the mirror out of the sink. I pressed a piece into her palm while I grasped the other. "Maybe now you will hear them too, maybe now you will know we are meant to be together."

"We are darling. We are. But let what we have now be enough for you. It has to be enough."

Our pale-blue eyes locked, we both knew it would never be enough. I wanted her close to me, touching me—more than that, I wanted to be inside her. God, even more than that—I wanted to be her.

In one fluid motion, we pierced each other in our awful, evil, pale-blue eyes with the shards from the mirror. The stars in the mirror, acting to part us forever like clandestine Romeo and Juliet.

I fell to the floor, my sister in my arms.

Blood, mingled with tears, rolled down her soft face. She looked just how she did as a child—her face small, her eyes large. "I couldn't let them send you away again."

I never felt more loved than I did in her arms. She feared I was mad and didn't want to see me locked away in the sanitarium again. She'd kill me to save me because she loves me. I, on the other hand, killed her to keep her because I couldn't bear to be separated from her. I couldn't bear her not being mine. I couldn't bear the idea of her leaving me for Eddy. I couldn't bear us not being alike.

But we weren't alike. She was the good in me and I was the evil in her. "God bless you, Sissy." With the last of my strength, I leaned in and kissed my sister goodbye. The taste of her blood on my lips, the trophy of my eternal guilt. "Oh, God bless you."

* * *

"Good God Kenneth! Are you okay?"

Eddy's voice stirred me from death. My face throbbed. I had been no stranger to pain, but this pain was unlike anything I'd experienced. It came from within, setting every nerve in my head on fire. My hand reached for my eye.

"Don't touch it," Eddy said. "We have to get you to a physician." He pulled me from the ground with the strength of two men. I leaned on the sink, avoiding my reflection in the mirror.

New tears formed in the corners of my eyes. My pale-blue eye stung under the burden. "Where's Sissy? Is she dead? Did I kill her?!" I pulled the shard of glass from my eye, my blood drenching my face in a red mask. I pressed my inner arm to it as a siege.

Folding his handkerchief into a square, Eddy pressed it to my eye. "Keep pressure on it." He grabbed my hand and pulled me in the direction of the door.

"I go nowhere until you tell me where Sissy is."

"Kenneth please, you need medical care."

I remained steadfast. I clenched my teeth in anger, biting back pain. "Tell me what you did with my sister! Where is she?!"

The idea that he whisked her away and I'd never see her again seized upon me. The smell of blood was becoming intoxicating. Emotion overflowed and I sobbed. "Please Eddy," I begged, leaning on the sink for support as my blood dripped into it in thick, rhythmic drops. "Don't take her from me."

I pawed at my face with my free hand, clearing away enough blood to see him. In his hand was my sister's red notebook.

I snatched it from him. "Sissy's book, why do you have it?! Where is she?!"

"That book is the reason I turned around," Eddy said, his countenance pale in the candle lit room. "I realized I'd walked out with it and wanted to return it. I know you write in it every day."

"What?—No, this is Sissy's book," I said, showing it to him, as if I hadn't just taken it from his hands. "She's the one who writes in it every day, not me. Where is she? Where's my twin sister?!"

A solitary tear rolled down his cheek. "She's been where she's been these last four years."

"What are you talking about?"

"Sissy is buried in Dahl Cemetery next to your mother."

His words shot an arrow through my heart. I nearly collapsed on the sink top. That wasn't possible. She was there with me in the bathroom. I had seen her, smelled her, touched her even. I could still remember the feel of my lips on hers, her satin dress between my fingers, my hands traveling up her legs.

"No," I said, standing strong on my two feet. I ripped the oval mirror off my lapel, letting the blood-soaked handkerchief fall to the floor. "Sissy gave me this for my birthday." I held it out for

Eddy to see as proof. "She gave me my birthday present, and I brought her here. I hurt her, Eddy. I'm sorry. I didn't mean to hurt her." I put the pin in my waistcoat pocket as I played back the evening aloud. "Then you came back to the house to return her book." I opened Sissy's notebook to see her scribbles of dam, dam, dam. I looked to Eddy. "She wants to be a poet like you, but she has writer's block."

"It *was* her book, Kenneth. Her favorite book, but you're the only one who writes in it now."

"Me?" *I knew myself no longer. My original soul seemed, at once, to take its flight from my body.* I glanced into the mirror, I needed to remember who Kenneth Live Dahl was. I scarcely recognized my own face, but I recognized the handwriting in the reflection. It was mine. Dam, dam, dam in the mirror read in my own shorthand: mad, mad, mad.

"No—this can't be true!"

I stormed out of the bathroom, tripping on the few steps on my climb up.

Eddy followed. "Where are you going?!"

I ran up the stairs, through the main hall and out the front entrance. Eddy ensued me to Dahl Cemetery. I ran through the gates not minding the beady-eyed ravens arched over it and ran to the west-end of the cemetery. The ground was wet, and my feet sank into the muddy earth with every step. The weather was still as if nothing dared to breathe. I fell to my knees in front of my sister's headstone.

'Here lies Ligeia Enola Dahl. Beloved Sissy to us all.'

I clawed at the marble plaque on the ground covering her body. "This is not real! This is not real!"

Eddy wrapped his arm around my shoulders. I trembled against him. "I thought you knew."

Peace had evaded me. Death had evaded me. Sissy was dead and I was alive and very much alone. I realized then, in a crowd of people, in a sea of voices, I would always be alone. *'From childhood's hour I have not been as others were-have not seen as others saw'* . . . Eddy was right, I was and am dammed.

I whimpered, sounding nothing like myself. All of the little tricks I had learned at the sanitarium had failed me. "What happened to her?"

"You fell down the stairs of your family's crypt. They found you lying in a pool of blood. Yours and Sissy's."

"You have it wrong. I remember that. I fell and Sissy went to get help."

He squeezed me to him. I could hear the thumping of his heart. "She never made it for help. Someone cut out her eye. She bled out before anyone found her."

"Oh God, no!" I pushed him away from me.

He wrangled me in, locking me in a hug. "She died Ken, but you survived."

I shook my head.

"We thought for a while we would lose you too. But you woke up, against all odds, you woke up. For a while you were your old self, but then you started acting strangely—withdrawn, despondent. I was on my way to visit Sissy's grave when I spotted you. I followed you because I was worried. I followed you into the potting shed. You dissected your grandmother's cat, Pluto, and many other strays. You had dug up Sissy and dissected her."

"No," I said, shaking my head violently while he held me, my tears a red river. The pain I felt was worse than anything I'd endured at Westminster. The fire that burned in my head was now in my heart consuming it, my every breath fueling the fire.

"You dug Sissy up and after that they sent you away."

"Oh Eddy . . . no . . ."

I pulled out the mirror pin from Sissy that I had tucked in my waistcoat pocket. I opened the back to read: Athena. It was hers, my Pallas Athena's. Sissy hadn't given it to me. She was never there. Her new portrait wasn't hung next to mine in the hall because she wasn't alive to have a new one painted. She died a thirteen-year-old little girl. I was the one who had been scribbling in Sissy's red notebook and tonight was no exception. That's why I lost track of time. I had wanted to be like Sissy, even be her and I was. I was Sissy and I was me. I tried to tell myself, by writing it out. But I didn't understand.

Athena said she didn't want to replace Sissy, but in a way she had. I had confused Athena with Sissy. Athena was the one who wrote to Eddy. She was the one Eddy was there to see. But she only had eyes for me, and she knew the truth about me. The very truth I scribbled in my sister's notebook.

That's why she didn't see the harm in giving me the mirror pin. She already knew I heard voices—Sissy's voice. She heard me speak to her and talk as her that first morning she brought me my breakfast and a daisy. My beloved Athena had protected me like Pallas Athena of old. My goddess of wisdom and war had kept my secret and kept me out of the Sanitarium.

Dr. Tarri was kinder than I gave him credit for. He let me keep my long hair because it reminded me of Sissy. He knew my twin sister had died and that it was digging her up that sent me to him, the voices being the culprit. My father had also let me keep my long hair on account of my dead, beloved sister. We *were* the last. It was just him and me, Sissy was dead. And now so was he. I was alone.

All the clues were there, and I had overlooked them. No—that wasn't true. I had deliberately ignored them. As Dr. Tarri knew,

I was sagacious. I was clever, too clever.

My hands rested on the marble plaque on the ground in front of my sister's tomb, as I looked toward the heavens. The starry sky of the mirror was high above me as blood dripped down my face into my mouth. I wasn't the sun. I was the demon who devoured it.

I laughed. My laugh pierced the silent night. The stone pavers placed over Athena's gravesite were to discourage me from unearthing her like I had unearthed Sissy. To ensure history didn't repeat itself.

"Eddy, it's the curse of the Dahls to only know Hell and the evil runs deeper than my eye. I could never have cut it out. The doctors never could have cured me, never could have rehabilitated me. It's who I am." I grabbed him by the shoulders. "Don't you see it now?! Don't you feel it, it's right beneath the surface. It's all true. Every last bit of it. There are no voices. I am truly and unequivocally insane. Sissy's dead. Our mother killed her. And I killed Athena."

Athena, who Eddy and I both loved. I had punished Eddy, but in doing so, I had punished myself, destroying my one chance at a happily ever after. I was and will always be the unassuming rosebush waiting to maim, blind, kill.

My blood-covered hands streaked down Eddy's face, cupping his head. "God bless you. Oh, God bless you. For anyone I love is damned."

Eddy fixated on my eye. He saw past the blood, past the pale-blue flesh and knew I spoke the truth. He murmured, "Lord help my poor soul."

The End . . .

Author's note:

"Lord help my poor soul," is rumored to have been Edgar Allan Poe's last words. Besides this Easter egg, *Eye of Athena* is packed with many other Poe Easter eggs, some obvious and some obscure. If you have not jumped down the Edgar Allan Poe rabbit-hole yet, I hope my story has inspired you to do so.

I drew inspiration for *Eye of Athena* from Edgar Allan Poe's real life and many of his works including but not limited to: *Alone, Annabel Lee, Eleonora, Ligeia, Marginalia, Mesmeric Revelation, Premature Burial, The Black Cat, The Cask of Amontillado, The Fall of the House of Usher, The Masque of the Red Death, The Narrative of Arthur Gordon Pym, The Pit and the Pendulum, The Raven, The Spectacles, The System of Doctor Tarr and Professor Fether* and *The Tell-Tale Heart.*

Want more Holly Knightley stories?

Find your next favorite story on my Amazon page now!

THANKS FOR READING!

If this book helped you escape, if only for a moment, please consider taking the time to leave a review or star rating on Amazon and all other platforms you use. It would warm the cockles of my little, black heart to hear from you.

Follow me on social media (I'm on all platforms under Holly Knightley). Sign up for my newsletter for the latest news, glimpse into my wacky process, and receive the occasional freebie. Stay spooky, and happy reading!